TRAILS TO LOVE

Marilyn Conner Miles

Copyright © 2014 Marilyn Conner Miles

All rights reserved

ISBN-13:978-1505299878

ISBN-10:150529987X

ACAPULCO ADVENTURE

> Diane, sorry, no juicy bits. Read it ANYWAY & write a REVIEW. Thanks, Marilyn

Brenda and the weatherman were right—the fog did clear up. In fact, the sun came out and nearly blinded me every time I looked out the big glass windows of the airport terminal where I worked as a ticket agent for WestAir. There were only a couple hours of my shift left and I checked the clock every few minutes.

I'd left home still feeling sorry for myself about the breakup with Mark. I wasn't in any shape to take this trip to Mexico. Brenda didn't understand. *She* had no trouble with men breaking up with her; she usually broke up with them. Still, I needed to be mature about it, so I put on my happy face.

I was in the middle of checking a passenger in, when I heard Brenda suck in a breath and say, "Uh-oh." A group of pilots stood around the ticket counter as usual chatting with her, but suddenly it got quiet, and when I looked up, I saw why: a few steps away from our counter, was Mark. And he wasn't alone. A blonde flight attendant stood next to him, her hand possessively holding onto his arm. I gave a horrified gasp, practically threw the ticket and change at the passenger, dashed away from the counter and stumbled into the back room.

I ran smack dab into a man's solid chest. "Ooof! Hey Dee, what's the hurry?"

I looked up. It was Greg, one of our pilots. "I, uh..."

But then I heard another familiar male voice. Mark must have seen my reaction and come after me. Maybe I'd over-reacted. Maybe that woman grabbed him and he was being polite. Maybe he was really looking for me and ran into her. Maybe he realized what a big mistake he'd made and wanted to get back together with me. All these thoughts ran through my mind in less than a second. There was only one way to show Mark that he didn't get under my skin.

I grabbed Greg by the shirt and pulled him down. I meant for the kiss to be a statement, but when he didn't pull away, it turned into something…good. Greg's arms that'd grabbed me when I ran into him, tightened around me, and pulled me closer.

When we finally broke apart, Mark watched us with the blonde still on his arm. Greg recuperated from the kiss much quicker than I did. Without missing a beat, he reached for Mark's hand and shook it. "Hey man, how are ya' doing? Long time no see."

"Well, it looks as though you're in good hands, Deeann. Uh, nice to see you guys again. We'd better get going. Come on, Suze," Mark said, and walked back out of the room, pulling the blonde after him.

"Why did you kiss me back?" I pushed away from Greg. "You just ruined my chances of ever getting back with him."

He watched me for a long moment before he replied, "I think I understand your motive for that kiss, but Dee, don't you see? Mark's already moved on."

Greg turned and left the room. I reached up and touched my lips, the feel of Greg's kiss still there.

After our shift ended, the three of us sat in the back room behind the counter, killing time until our flights out. Greg was engrossed in a game of Solitaire, which left Brenda and me time to talk.

"That's it. I've had it. No more men for me. You can say, 'I told you so' if you want, but I'm glad you talked me into taking this trip after all," I admitted sheepishly. "In fact, I'm really looking forward to some girl time. No men."

"Uh, yeah, well about that..." she began hesitantly, and looked over at Greg.

I looked at her with suspicion. "What? Is there something you're not telling me?"

"Well, remember, you told me to find someone else to go with me. And you know how much I've been looking forward to this trip...and well, it sounded as though you were going to flake out on me...so I asked Greg and he said yes," she finished in a rush of words. Before I could respond, she rose from the chair and said, "I'm going outside for a smoke." She left in a hurry.

Greg shuffled the cards as I crossed my legs and anxiously bounced my foot.

"Are you looking forward to the trip?" I asked Greg as he picked up his cards.

"With you?" He winked. Greg was always a flirt. With his dark brown hair and darker eyes, he was handsome, and our tailored polyester airline uniforms emphasized his broad shoulders and chest. But the last thing I needed right now was another boyfriend.

"Yes...no. We are going to Mexico together, but not *together*."

"Whatever you say. A little fun in the sun. Come on Dee, you hafta' learn how to have a little fun."

"I *am* fun." I frowned. Everyone thought I was fun. Well, maybe I wasn't my usual fun self since this thing with Mark...

Greg cocked his head to listen to an announcement over the intercom. "Come on, that's us." He scooped up the cards and shoved them into his backpack. "I'll get Brenda."

"Okay, I'll catch up." Why was I always rattled when I was around him? Just because I'd kissed him didn't mean that I *liked* him. He was like Mark, flirting with every female in sight. I sighed and reached down to pick up my purse, carry-on bag and suitcase. Because we travelled standby, I didn't check the suitcase ahead of time. It wasn't there. Greg must have picked it up and taken it for me. Just in case, I searched around some more, but I heard the crackle of the intercom announcing the second call for our flight. I rushed out the door and down the corridor to the gate where Brenda waved frantically at me

"Hurry! Greg's already boarded," she called.

We were the last passengers to board the plane and lucky to find seats next to each other. I saw Greg down the aisle. Before I could ask him about my suitcase, a flight attendant came by offering drinks.

"To fun and excitement," Brenda said, and lifted her glass in a toast. I clinked my glass of Seven and Seven with hers, and then downed it. When I looked back at Greg again, I saw him chatting with the pretty female flight attendant. I happened to glance over the flight attendant's shoulder and noticed a dark-complexioned man looking at them with a glare. Maybe he was impatient for his drink. He wore a deep scowl on his somewhat puffy face, and his cheap suit looked ill-fitting and un-pressed. His hair fell in greasy strands across his forehead, and he constantly reached up to push them aside.

When I turned back, Brenda had already drifted off to sleep, so I pulled my newest romance novel out of my carry-on bag and began to read.

I jerked awake when I felt something cold and wet land on me. The liquid dripped down my neck and soaked the front of my uniform blouse.

"Oh, I'm so sorry, Miss. I didn't see your feet in the aisle." The flight attendant handed me a towel and I dabbed at my neck and clothing. I knew it was already too late. The dark, red wine stained the cloth. Since I didn't have my bag, I wouldn't be able to change into something clean and dry until we reached our final destination. I turned in my seat and looked down the aisle to Greg, remembering that I wanted to ask him about my suitcase.

"Greg," I whispered loudly, but his eyes were closed and he looked as though he was asleep. I sighed. Nothing I could do about it now. I'd have to wait till we got to Los Angeles to ask him.

We had a four-hour layover in Los Angeles until we caught our early morning connecting flight to Acapulco. The airport was quiet. We passed by small groups of sleeping travellers sprawled across the uncomfortable chrome and vinyl waiting area chairs, their belongings spread around them like settlers in a fort holed up against attack. Brenda and I headed straight to a restroom, to see if we could get some of the stain off my blouse. Greg disembarked the plane before we did, and I saw him headed to the shops.

As we left the restroom, Brenda startled me by asking, "What's he doing?"

"Who?" I turned my head to see who she referred to and saw Greg down on his hands and knees on the floor. A young woman with long, bleached-blonde hair, stood next to him, biting at the fingernails on her left hand, with a worried look on her face. She looked pretty, in an artificial way, with her tight designer jeans, high open-toed wedge shoes and tube top.

Greg looked up and cried, "Stand back!" We stopped abruptly and I looked at the blonde for an explanation.

"I lost a contact," she said simply and then ignored us as we stood there, unable to move lest we step on it. Then she plucked something out of her plunging neckline and giggled. "Oh gosh, here it is. I'm so sorry I put you to all that trouble," she said to Greg in a sugary-sweet voice.

He rose from the floor, dusting the dirt off his cream-colored uniform slacks and then his hands. "Oh that's all right. No trouble at all." He smiled at her.

Before he could say more to her, I cut in and asked, "Did you check my bag all the way through?"

"Me? Why would I check your bag?" He looked confused.

I frowned. "Didn't you take it with you to the gate? It wasn't in the back room when I looked."

"I took it down to the gate for you, but I figured you'd check it in when we got the okay to fly. Didn't you see it on the floor where we waited?"

"No, I was late, 'cause I tried to find my bag, and when I got to the gate, Brenda said you'd already boarded, so I assumed you'd checked it for me. You mean you didn't? My voice rose. "So where is it?"

"Uh, maybe still at Sea-Tac?" Greg looked sheepish.

"All I have to wear now is what I have on?" I gestured.

"Maybe you could wear some of my clothes," Brenda offered.

"Thanks, but I'll find something when we get to Acapulco," I told her. *Yeah right. She was a size eight and I was a twelve. What else could go wrong on this vacation?*

The first thing I noticed when we stepped off the plane in Acapulco was the oppressive heat. Sweat trickled down my forehead. Our polyester uniforms kept us warm in the chilly dawn of Los Angeles in October, but in this tropical climate, they were too much. I could hardly wait to get some cooler clothes.

We finally made it through Customs—at least I'd kept my tourist card in my purse—then Greg and I helped Brenda drag her three large suitcases outside the airport terminal into the blazing sun and hailed one of the beat-up, windowless cabs.

"Holiday Inn," Greg told the driver.

"*Sí, sí.*" The cabbie gave us a sparse-toothed grin. I don't know where he learned to drive. If the cab even *had* brakes, he didn't use them. The car hurtled along the narrow, cliff-hugging roads with barely room enough for one vehicle, let alone two. I looked at Brenda and the fear in her eyes probably mirrored mine. I would have closed my eyes but didn't want to miss out on the view. There was a spectacular picture-perfect view—the breathtakingly beautiful city of Acapulco set on a semi-circular bay, flanked by the Sierra

Madres. The aquamarine bay and un-crowded white beaches were surrounded by elegant modern multi-storied hotels, flanked with palm trees and swimming pools. I'd learned from my guidebook that Acapulco was the nation's oldest and best-known resort, often called, "the pearl of the Pacific."

After we checked into our luxurious rooms where signs on the water faucets warned us "don't drink the water," I headed for the beach with Brenda and Greg in my bare feet. I'd managed to find some short shorts and a top that barely fit, in the hotel's small and *expensive* gift shop— why did they think only *small* women needed beach wear? Now my budget was shot from buying clothes I hadn't planned to spend money on. I'd put back the sandals that would've fit me, and settled for some practical shoes I could wear everywhere. I should have worn them down from the room because the white sand burned. I ran to one of the thatched umbrellas, threw my hotel room towel onto the shaded sand under it, and leaped onto it.

At night, the city came alive. Every grand hotel offered nightly entertainment, including the dance-till-dawn discos. Our first night there, strolling musicians playing acoustic guitars serenaded us while we dined in the hotel's outdoor restaurant and then we listened to a small mariachi band.

"Isn't this romantic?" Brenda sighed. "This would be a great place for a honeymoon."

I merely nodded.

Greg suggested, "Let's try the nightclub on the hotel's top floor." Before we could even look at the menu and choose our drinks, the waiter came over with three huge margaritas the size of fishbowls. "These are from Señor Alvarez with his compliments." He tipped his head in the direction of a large round table nearby.

Brenda smiled over at the man seated there and mouthed, "Thank you."

He stood and walked toward us.

"What should I say?" Brenda whispered. "I don't speak Spanish."

Before I could answer, he'd reached our table, and looking at Brenda, asked in perfect English, "May I?" When she nodded, he pulled up a chair, sat down and stared at her. "My name is Ricardo Alvarez. Welcome to Acapulco." He spoke to all of us, but looked at Brenda. He waved the waiter over and ordered a chilled bottle of champagne.

It was nice to have a high-powered accountant like Ricardo in our company; he got top attention and service at the hotels. The next evening, he asked the three of us to the most elaborate and popular discotheque in town, *La Danza*. It was brightly-lit by multi-colored neon lights that flashed to the music's beat, and packed with people of all nationalities. Greg joined the dancing throng and Brenda and Ricardo got up to dance too.

Ricardo politely asked me to dance with him, but I knew he'd rather be with Brenda, so I made up some excuse not to. I could see the relief on his face, as he turned then to Brenda and smiled.

"Are you sure, Dee?" Brenda asked. She must be worried that I wasn't having fun. She looked around. "Where's Greg?"

I waved my hand in the direction of the crowded dance floor. "Over there. He hasn't let the language barrier stop him. You go have fun. I'll just enjoy my drink and soak up the atmosphere to remember when we get back home."

"Well okay, if you're sure—" But Ricardo grabbed her hand and led her off to dance.

I sat at the one of the two small tables pushed together, and stared at the gyrating bodies dancing to the beat of KC and the Sunshine Band's *"Get Down Tonight,"* under the spinning disco ball. *The 70s were alive and well in Mexico.* I would have liked to dance—if I knew how.

Greg came back to our table then, and held out his hand to me. "Ready to dance?"

"Uhh..." I thought quickly. "If I had the right clothes, I'd love to. But I could only afford to buy one nice dress at the gift shop and it doesn't exactly fit. I'm afraid if I dance, it will come apart at the seams right out there on the dance floor."

"Sure, I can see what you mean. That dress *is* pretty tight," he replied, eyeing me up and down. "But I have no complaints. Hey, listen. They're playing our song, 'Dance With Me' by Orleans." He grabbed my hand and pulled me up, obviously determined to ignore my stalling methods. "I won't do anything fancy. Come on, you gotta have fun sometime."

I'd step on his feet. At least with a fast song, I could probably fake it. I mentally kicked myself for letting him pull me out here.

"Smile, Dee. You look way too serious. We're here to have fun, remember?" Greg said as he took me in his arms.

I looked around at the other couples on the dance floor. I tried to remember what my dad practiced with me when I was a teenager, before I went to my first school dance. I'd danced little since then.

"Relax," Greg coaxed in my ear. He led me around the floor to the rhythm of the music, but I knew I must look stiff and awkward.

"I guess I'm a little rusty."

"Don't worry about it." He moved my arms so they were around his neck, and put his around my waist. "Just close your eyes and relax. Let yourself feel the music."

With his arms around me, and my eyes closed, I finally relaxed. His aftershave smelled yummy. Acqua di Gio? Yum. I opened my eyes briefly to find his warm brown gaze looking down into mine. I smiled and he pulled me even closer, and dipped his head. I raised mine to meet him with the anticipation of his lips on mine...

Rippppp.

"Oh no!" I gasped at the sight of the side seam of my dress split wide open.

Greg grinned and looked me up and down, probably enjoying the show. "I could have guessed that you had more curves than that dress could handle."

I glared. "Is that a compliment or an insult?"

"Definitely a compliment."

I punched his arm. "Walk in front of me to the ladies' room, will you, and then tell Brenda I need her help."

When we reached the restroom door, I stepped inside, and saw Brenda there. I turned back to tell Greg, but he'd already walked halfway back to our table and wouldn't be able to hear me over the music. Then I saw that there was another man sitting at the table with Ricardo. I'd seen him at the nightclub the night we met Ricardo, but he'd only walked in, spoken to Ricardo briefly and left. This time they were engrossed in conversation. He looked up when Greg approached, said something, then stood up and headed for the exit door.

"So tell me, what's going on with you and Greg? I saw you two out there on the dance floor," Brenda asked, and smiled at me. I turned back to face her and she saw my ruined dress for the first time. "Oh my. Dee, what happened?"

"Greg insisted that I dance with him and my dress blew up."

"Here," Brenda said as she dug into her purse. "I have safety pins." She helped me pull the sides together.

"Thanks, Bren, you're a lifesaver." As we headed back to our table, I added, "But I won't be dancing any more tonight."

Before we reached our table I felt surprised to spot the man who'd tried to get the flight attendant's attention on the first leg of our trip. A feeling of uneasiness ran up my spine.

"Dee, why did you stop?"

The man saw us staring at him, and he glared back.

"Do you know that guy?" Brenda asked.

"Not really. Let's hurry back before we lose the table," I said. I felt the man's gaze as we walked by.

Ricardo suggested we three take a boat cruise the next evening since he had to work. The pamphlet promised we would see the "world famous, death-defying" cliff divers at

La Quebrada who plunged 130 feet into the Pacific Ocean. We saw the cliffs, but not the divers. The diving ended for the day by the time we got there. I felt disappointed about not seeing the cliff divers and meant to tell Ricardo about it, since he told us it was one of the most popular tourist attractions we shouldn't miss during our stay.

A swarthy man dressed as a pirate, ran around on the deck brandishing a sword and posing with the tourists—for a fee, of course. He sat down next to me and I turned away to look at Brenda with dismay as I tried unsuccessfully to move closer to her and away from him. His breath smelled bad and his hair looked oily and he put his arm around me.

"Oh come on, Dee," Brenda urged me. "Pose for the photographer. Another memory for your scrapbook."

I knew she referred to all the photos I'd taken on our vacation so far. "Oh, okay," I agreed reluctantly, though I cringed inside. I smiled half-heartedly while the photographer took the picture, but I felt glad when he left. I rubbed my hands up and down over my arms, as though that could take away the pirate's touch. I must have looked as though I was cold; since the sun was beginning to set, the air had grown cooler.

"Cold?" Greg asked as he sat down on the other side of me.

"Yeah, it is a bit chilly. I wish I'd brought my shawl, but it was so hot when we left the hotel. This sleeveless dress was perfect then."

"Maybe I can help. My shirt has long sleeves and I'm plenty warm." He reached out his arm and put it around me. "If you don't mind..."

Mind? Oh no. This felt nothing like the pirate's arm around me. We were so close I could feel his breath on my cheek. I moved into his warmth and he hugged me close. "Mmmmm," I said, feeling the warmth of him spread through me. Then I pulled back abruptly and sat up. He had a girlfriend! No matter how much I might want to, I shouldn't be doing this with him. "Greg..."

"Hmmm?"

"Brenda told me you have a girlfriend."

"What?" He looked around me at Brenda, but she was chatting to a woman on the other side of her. "Oh, uh, yeah her."

"Why didn't she come on this trip with you?"

"She...she...had to work."

"What does she look like? Do I know her?"

"I doubt it. She's uhhh..." He looked as though he was trying to remember. "Oh, she's about five-foot seven, I guess, long, dark brown hair and eyes..."

"What does she do for a living? Does she work for the airlines too?"

"Yeah, she's a ticket agent."

"Gosh, Greg, it sounds like you could be describing me. I'll have to meet her sometime. Well, uh, thanks for warming me up," I said and stood up. "I think I'll take a walk around the boat."

"Want me to go with you?" he asked.

"No, that's okay, but thanks." I walked away, but when I turned and looked back, Greg and Brenda seemed to be arguing, and Greg was frowning.

Later, as we disembarked from the boat, I turned around to get one last look at the bay in the warm moonlit night air. I'd come back the next day, if I could, to take a picture of it surrounded by the Sierra Madre Mountains, in the daylight. I gasped and stopped so suddenly that Greg, behind me, bumped into me.

"Why did you stop?" he asked me. That's when I began to wonder if I was imaging things. A man stood at the bottom of the ramp talking to the pirate and he looked like the same unpleasant man from the plane and cocktail lounge. Why did he keep appearing at the same places as us? Greg didn't give me time to answer his question. "Dee! You're holding up the line behind us. We need to keep moving."

I looked again while we waited for a taxi to take us back to the hotel, but by then, the man disappeared.

Again, I decided not to tell Brenda or Greg about it. They would tease me about my over-active imagination. I always had my head in a book on my breaks at work, and Brenda told me that I should write my own novel someday. They would probably think my fears were all in my head— or something like that—so I kept my creepy feelings to myself.

Brenda didn't feel good the next morning. She said she'd been sick all night, so Greg and I went out to shop in the open air market, Mercado Municipal.

"*Buenas días, señorita,*" an older woman greeted us when we walked into her shop and I began to look at white peasant blouses with colorful embroidery.

"I don't like to haggle," I whispered to Greg.

He held up a hand, and then said to the woman, "I'll give you thirty pesos for this, *señora.*"

"No, no, *señor*. Sixty *pesos.*"

I reached for my purse, but Greg pushed my hand away.

"Wait. Don't you need a skirt to go with it?"

I nodded.

"I'll take care of this."

I'd wandered over to look at some leather wallets when Greg strode toward me. He looked pleased. "I talked her down and she sold me both the blouse *and* a colorful red and black skirt to match. It was only fifty *pesos*." I reached into my purse to get the money, but he stayed my hand and shook his head. "No, Dee. Keep your money. It's my fault you have to get more clothes. I left your suitcase behind and then I practically danced the only dress you have off you last night. Please, it's the least I can do."

"I bit my lip. The gesture was awfully nice and I could tell he still felt bad.

"Come on, please Dee? Let me do this, or I'll think you're still mad at me. I won't be able to enjoy this vacation."

"Okay, just so we're squared up now."

"You're not mad at me anymore?"

"No."

"Good." He reached one arm out and gave me a hug. For a few minutes, it almost felt like a date. I thought about the kiss in the back office before we left and the hug just now and on the boat...and the girlfriend. All of a sudden, I didn't care. I felt reckless today. When Greg grabbed my hand and pulled me up the alley to the next shop, I didn't protest.

Unfortunately, our pleasant outing was short-lived. When I unlocked the door, Brenda was in the bathroom, violently ill. I turned and ran down the hall to Greg's room, and pounded on the door.

"We need to get Brenda to the hospital. She's really sick!"

When he opened the door, he was bare-chested and his hair was damp on the ends, I supposed, from just getting out of the shower. I glanced at him briefly, and wished I had a few more minutes to enjoy the view.

"I'll call the front desk and make sure a taxi is waiting. Do you think we can get her down the stairs?"

"We can sure try."

The doctor found us seated in the crowded waiting room when he came out to give us Brenda's diagnosis. He spoke rapid-fire Spanish which I barely understood. I sat there and felt helpless. A nurse must have spotted us. When the doctor left, she came over and explained in English.

"Your friend has food poisoning. She will need to take medicine the doctor prescribed, and shots, twice a day. Your hotel can help with this, but she needs to stay in bed."

When Greg and I walked into Brenda's room she rolled over on the bed to face us. "I'm so sorry, guys," she said. "I feel as though I've let you down, and spoiled the whole trip."

"You can't help it," I tried to assure her.

"I don't want you to miss the trip to Taxco, tomorrow."

"Why don't we postpone it? Maybe you'll be better in a couple days and feel up to going." I took her hand in hopes it would make her feel better.

"No." She shook her head. "I've already ruined this vacation enough for you. You need to go with Greg."

I looked at Greg.

"We'll go," he said. "You just get better."

The next morning, I went to the concierge desk and asked them to recommend a good car rental agency. The clerk immediately replied, "Rentabug."

I thought he didn't understand me. I repeated my question, louder and slower this time: "No…we need…a …car."

He shook his head and wrote it down on a page of the hotel stationery for me. Sure enough, that's what he'd said. I frowned, but before I could say anything more Greg came bounding up to the counter on his tennis shoe-clad feet.

"What's the matter?" he asked. He must have seen my frown. I showed him the paper. Greg broke into laughter. "Bug. You know, a Volkswagen: Rent-A-Bug."

"Oh." I looked up at the desk clerk. He smiled broadly.

"*Sí, sí.*" He nodded, several times.

We finally got the rental car and drove into the country. The scenery changed abruptly as soon as we began the climb out of the city. Instead of high-rise hotels, discos and sandy beaches, bleak little shacks crowded the hillsides, where children, pigs and dogs ran, played or scratched in the dirt. I'd brought my camera along and at first, I felt hesitant to take pictures, afraid an angry mob would attack the car and send us hurtling over the side of the road and down the cliffs. But all I saw were children and old women herding heavily-burdened donkeys along the road, or pigs and roosters strolling fearlessly across our path.

The scenery changed again as we got closer to Taxco, and became more desert-like. Greg slowed the car when, up ahead, we spotted a small one-story building. It looked like an abandoned gas station. It was the only sign of life we'd seen for miles, since we'd entered the desert.

There were no other cars around when we pulled up in front, but a couple of scowling Mexican men, smoking cigarettes, squatted under the adobe structure's only window. One of them looked familiar...the man from the plane, cocktail lounge and boat? It *couldn't* be him. I *was* paranoid. Nevertheless, I grabbed Greg's arm nervously when he prepared to leave the car.

"What's the matter?" he asked.

"Let's not go in there."

"Why not?"

"It gives me the creeps," I mumbled.

"If you don't want to go, I'll get something for us to drink. I'll be right back." He gave me an amused look.

"No! Don't leave me here alone!" I cried in a panic. I quickly opened the passenger door, slid out, and then locked it. I clutched my shoulder bag to my side. Greg stopped and looked back as I jogged to catch up with him.

"You sure are nervous," he said. "Either you watch too many movies or you have quite the imagination." He laughed.

I sighed. "Let's hurry so we can get back on the road." He didn't say anything, only looked at me and shook his head, then walked into the store.

The last fifty miles passed without further incident and we arrived safely in Taxco. The desert-like terrain had changed to hills and mountains. Taxco was known as "The Silver Center of the World," and lay spread out over a scenic hillside, part of the Sierra Madre range of mountains. At the top of the steep road that lead into Taxco, the road divided. As we tried to determine which way to go, a man waved at us, in front of a long, one-story building made of white adobe. A sign on the building had "Information" printed on it.

"*Buenas dias, Bienvenidos a Taxco.* Good day and welcome to Taxco. My name is *Señor Pildago.* I am a member of the Chamber of Commerce. How may I assist you?

"We've just come from Acapulco for the day. We heard that there are silver mines and shops," I said.

He gave us a quick history of the town. "It's one of the oldest colonial cities in Mexico with rich silver deposits, and it was declared a National Colonial Monument in 1928," he bragged. "We're known as Mexico's 'Silver City.'" Along with the brochures and maps he gave us, he told us about silver shops selling handmade jewellery, and leather goods shops. "But stay away from the lower part of town," he warned us. "They charge higher prices and they'll cheat you."

"Where's a good place to stay tonight?" Greg asked him.

"Something nice, but inexpensive," I added.

"Well, the best place to stay is the Holiday Inn, however"—he spread out his hands and shrugged his shoulders—"it isn't cheap. But a nice young couple such as yourselves...you don't want to stay just anywhere. Perhaps it's your honeymoon?"

I blushed. Why did he assume that since we travelled together, we were anything more than friends? I looked to Greg to supply the answer.

"No," was all he said.

"Would you like me to call and make a reservation for you?" *Señor Pildago* asked. When Greg nodded, he disappeared behind the curtain. He returned a few minutes later and said, "It's all arranged. Enjoy your time here in Taxco."

We thanked him and got back into the car, following his directions to the motel he'd found for us. The road was steep, narrow, winding cobblestone, barely wide enough for a car, let alone bicycles. It was made even narrower by donkeys, goats, pigs and pedestrians. The streets were lined with old homes with intricately carved door and ornate ironwork. I ohhed and ahhed over the homes and their colorful flower-filled patios. "We must be at the very top of Taxco, by now," I said, pulling out my camera. "We should have a good view of the town from the motel."

"There it is—I think." Greg pointed out the window. I looked at the long, rambling building with a crumbling, faded sign. It was hard to read the words on it, but it was the only building around that in any way resembled a hotel or motel. The rest of the buildings were merely shacks.

"Pildago said to follow the street to the end, didn't he? This is definitely the end."

I stared at it in dismay. "The paint's all peeling off."

"Oh, is that paint?" Greg joked.

"I don't know about this one. Can't we try some other place?"

"You heard the man. This is the only affordable place with a vacancy. He ought to know. Besides, if we don't hurry and check in, it'll be too late to see the shops before they close."

"I guess you're right, but—"

"You're not used to roughing it. You can't expect AAA's 'excellent' rating every place you go."

"Yeah, but I bet AAA doesn't even *know* about this place." I got out of the car and walked to the hotel door.

A large woman dressed all in black, rose somewhat reluctantly it seemed from behind a counter when we walked into what appeared to be the office. Through the open door behind her, I could see an unmade bed and a television atop a tiny refrigerator. The television squawked loudly, but she made no attempt to turn it down.

"*Dos Cuartos, por favor*, two rooms please," I said to her. It was hard to understand what she said, with the noise and her lack of the English language.

"No, *no tengo cuarto*, we don't have a room." The woman scowled and shook her head.

"But Señor Pidalgo—"

At the sound of his name, she smiled. "*Oh, sí. Sí, sí, sí, Señor Pidalgo! Bien.*" She pushed a register toward Greg. "*Escribe su nombre aqui*," she said, then handed him a pen and showed him where to sign his name. She didn't seem to care whether I signed it or not. Then she led us to a room at the farthest end of a dark, musty-smelling hall. Opening the door, she smiled and waddled off down the corridor in the direction we'd come. I stared at the two narrow cot-like beds, the dark dresser with a spindly wooden chair and the faded, worn upholstered chair next to a small, chipped, black-lacquered nightstand and lamp.

"I told her we needed *two* rooms," I said to Greg in dismay.

"Okay, I'll go back and see if I can talk to her about getting another room."

While he left, I walked to the window to see the view. Maybe I could get a good picture of the city from there. I pulled the curtain aside and to my amazement, there was no real window, only a painting that portrayed a scene someone would see if they *had* a window to look out. I didn't even know the name of the motel—Señor Alvarez hadn't told us, and the sign was impossible to read from the car when we arrived.

Greg came back. "The office was closed. I wandered around a bit, but couldn't find the manager—or anyone at all, actually. This place is weird."

I almost didn't care that we had to share the room. I wasn't so sure that I wanted to be alone in that room at night anyway. I showed him the 'window.'

"Someone's strange idea of interior decorating, I guess." He laughed and shrugged.

I told him once again how I felt about the place, but he merely patted my shoulder and seemed to humor me. "You'll feel better once you've eaten, and if it still bothers you that much, we'll ask at the restaurant for another place to stay. Come on, let's find someplace to eat." He attempted to lock the door before we left, but I noticed that it didn't completely close. I tried to push the door open from the hallway, but it wouldn't. I supposed it was locked then, but it didn't seem very secure.

Greg was already half-way down the hall before he must've noticed I wasn't behind him. "What are you doing?"he called.

"The door—it's—oh, never mind." I hurried down the corridor after him.

We found a charming restaurant atop a pottery shop. The building was all white adobe with a rippling red tile roof. We sat outside on a balcony which afforded us a good view of the alley below and the roofs of the buildings on either side. Red clay pots of dead flowers perched precariously on the low, narrow, red brick wall that prevented us from falling down onto the street. Even though the sun sunk lower in the sky, the air still felt oppressively hot and humid. I felt sluggish and sleepy after the long drive and the heat and could happily have laid my head down on the table and slept. But I kept myself awake by slapping at the flies that buzzed noisily around my face and landed on my arms.

We sat there for a long while before the lone waiter appeared to discover us. He came over carrying a large jug of water which he poured into glasses for us, then handed out thick paper menus. I felt relieved to find he had a good grasp of the English language. At least ordering our meal shouldn't take much of an effort.

I studied Greg as he looked over the menu. He looked tired too. His usually perfectly styled hair lay in damp, limp strands across his forehead.

After we ordered, we couldn't seem to find much to say to each other, which I blamed on our condition rather than my lack of wit and fluent conversational expertise.

After dinner, we went off to play tourist. We walked back to where Greg parked the car, in front of the impressively ornate Santa Prisca Catholic Church. I'd seen the church's twin towers and round dome since we'd arrived in town. It was all brick, a creamy, almost golden-with-age color. The church was surrounded by a ten-foot high curlicue black wrought-iron fence.

"I want to get a picture of this. Would you pose in front, please?"

"Nah, I'd feel silly—like a tourist."

"You *are* a tourist," I reminded him, and he finally obliged.

We passed a vendor on the street selling brightly-colored hammocks made out of a kind of twine-like rope. I thought they were over-priced. Greg bought three. "I hope you have a lot of trees on your property," I told him.

"I plan to build a house. I'll need them."

I wondered if the girlfriend would help him.

When we came out of the last shop, the air still hadn't cooled. It was getting dark, though, and most of the shops were closing. An elderly man pushed a cart along trying to sell the last of his wares.

"Popsicles! Let's get one." My mouth still burned from the spiciness of the Mexican food.

"Yeah, okay."

I found my favorite flavor—lime. The flavored ice numbed my lips and slipped coolly down my burning throat as we walked down the winding street, past the darkened shops and to the car. I wouldn't have made the walk alone. I moved a little closer to Greg. "We didn't get to the silver mine and gift shop Señor Pidalgo said we *must* see. I could get some good silver jewellery," I told him.

He didn't reply. I turned and saw a pained look on his face.

"You look awful. What's the matter?"

"I'm not sure," he replied. "Maybe all this spicy food is getting to me. They make it a little hotter here than I'm used to."

I could tell he didn't feel well. The pained expression didn't go away. His arms were full of his purchases and some of mine he'd insisted on carrying.

"Here, let me take those."

But I got from him was a brief, half-hearted, "No" before he reluctantly surrendered them to me. Then he jerked as a painful spasm jolted him and he wrapped his arms around his body almost hugging himself. He staggered over to an adobe wall. I quickly shifted all the packages to my right arm and hand and with my left I reached out and grabbed his elbow to keep him from falling.

Greg's symptoms looked alarmingly to me like Brenda's when she came down with food-poisoning. But she'd been able to go to bed and lay down. Greg and I were still on a darkened street quite a ways from the car and I didn't know where we would get help.

"Why don't we stop awhile and rest?"

He grunted, which seemed to mean 'yes,' so I steered him over to the side of the building where he could sit on the sidewalk and lean against the wall. I sat too and wondered what to do next. Should I leave him and get the car? But that meant me walking the street alone and I hated to leave him in his pitiful state. He would be easy prey. I considered asking him what he thought I should do, but I doubted he was up to making any kind of decision. It was up to me.

I decided we should try to walk to the car. I stuck out a hand to pull him to his feet. He chose to ignore it with an even-though-I'm-on-my-deathbed-I'm-still-tough, attitude, and pushed up off the sidewalk. He staggered away from the wall, bent over like a man hunched against the driving snow and wind of a blizzard. I reached for his elbow again, but he cried out, "Don't touch me!"

I yanked my hand away and stepped back, unable to conceal my hurt feelings. I felt tears flood my eyes, yet at the same time, I felt angry too. Sure he was sick, but I was tired

Greg must have seen the expression on my face, or realized how ungrateful he'd sounded. "Look, I'm sorry, but I can't bear being touched right now. I've never felt so—" he broke off, and stumbled to the gutter. I knew he needed to see a doctor, and made a decision.

"Greg, I need to go get the car."

He jerked his head up. "No!" Don't leave me—please."

"Greg, the car can't be too far away. I'll—"

"Please?"

Aw, I'm a sucker for that word. "Okay, okay."

We made slow progress down the street. At least it was all downhill. All the shops were closed by then. A sudden, unwanted thought occurred to me and made me even more uneasy: maybe we were in such a high crime area that people were afraid to walk the street alone at night. I didn't even see a dog or cat sniffing through the garbage. We stopped now and then for Greg to throw up. It *almost* didn't bother me anymore, and despite his aversion to being touched when he felt ill, I took a Kleenex from my bag and wiped his damp face and pushed the sweat-drenched hair out of his eyes.

"Thanks." He smiled weakly.

Abruptly, in the light of the full moon, I saw something move in a darkened shop doorway. I froze, and pulled Greg to a stop with me. He looked up. "Are we there?"

I held a finger to my lips. "Shh."

"Why?"

"I saw something move over there," I whispered, and pointed.

"It's probably some animal."

"Probably," I muttered. But what *kind* of animal? Whatever, we had to keep moving. I started forward again, but my heart pounded abnormally and my hand was about as damp as Greg's shirtsleeve that I still held. When we came up even with the doorway, I think my heart almost stopped and I gasped as I jerked Greg's arm.

A man stepped in front of us. He appeared to be studying us. My heartbeat kicked up. His yellowed teeth were uneven and there were a couple gaps where he had no teeth at all. It was the man dressed as a pirate on the boat cruise. But this time, he wasn't wearing the pirate's outfit he'd worn on the boat. He moved from the doorway toward us. *Oh no, this is exactly what I was afraid of*, I thought hopelessly, and if possible, my heart beat even faster. If he tried to harm Greg, I'd-I'd...

Nothing happened. The guy stopped. What was with him?

"Hospital?" I asked tentatively, hopefully.

He finally spoke. "No," he said, and shrugged his shoulders, then moved away.

"No? What did he mean by that? There has to be a doctor or hospital someplace around here," I said to Greg, frustrated and angry. I looked down at Greg for a moment and when I looked up again, the man had gone—vanished into the darkness. Could it be my spooked imagination played tricks on me and I'd only imagined him, as I probably imagined that other unpleasant fellow on the boat speaking to him? Why would that pirate be in Taxco?

I pulled Greg along as fast as I could, no longer afraid of the empty, dark street, but only of what tricks my mind might play on me again.

We finally reached the car, and I realized, horrified, that *I'd* have to drive it. I hadn't driven a car with a stick-shift in years. And then, I only had a couple lessons, so I never really got good at it. "It's like learning to ride a bike; once you do it, you never forget how," I mumbled aloud. "I hope."

I got Greg settled into the passenger seat, where his head flopped back against the headrest, his eyes closed, and then I climbed into the driver's side.

I looked at the stick and remembered the **H** position, but which gear was which? I studied the pedals, trying to remember which was the clutch and which the brake. At least I didn't have to back up out of our parking spot. I hoped to ease the car out onto the road—if I didn't kill it. I glanced nervously at Greg, whose eyes were still closed. Then, pressing my left foot hard onto the clutch pedal and my right on the brake, I eased the stick from neutral into first, and hoped I hadn't stripped the gears. But other than a little jerk, the car rolled fairly smoothly onto the road. Great.

Now, which one was second? When was I supposed to shift again? I tried to remember what I'd been taught by my high school boyfriend. And then, oh-my-gosh it was there before me: a goat standing in the road. I would have to stop, but I didn't know how. Should I step on the brake? Didn't I have to shift down? Was I supposed to step on the clutch? *Oh damn, wake up Greg.*

I felt shaken when we reached the motel. I'd stepped hard on the brakes, the car died and coasted to a stop—inches from the goat. It looked at the car then slowly walked away. I waited a minute or two with my head on the wheel, trying to calm down from all the adrenaline that kicked in. I looked over at Greg and this time, felt glad he was asleep. I managed to get the car started and we continued on.

The motel appeared as strangely quiet as ever, and awfully dark. I realized then something that I hadn't noticed before—there weren't any other cars parked in front of it, not even the manager's. The manager. Maybe the shift had changed and the night manager could tell me where to find a doctor.

I pulled Greg out of the car, and dragged him to the motel's front door, then left him momentarily propped against a pillar. If I had to get him back in the car to drive to a hospital, it would be easier that way.

I walked into the lobby and noticed immediately the large woman wasn't there. The door behind the counter was still open, but the room was dark. I looked at my watch. It *was* very late. I considered pounding on a service bell to wake someone up, but couldn't see one.

I walked back outside and found Greg on the ground in a heap, asleep. I struggled to awaken him and wished there was someone around to help me. I pushed and prodded at him. The man was solid as a rock wall. I hated to wake him up—sleep was what he needed. "We're at the motel, Greg. I need to get you to the room."

"Leave me here. It's...okay," he croaked as he began to slide from my precarious grip.

"No. You can't stay here." I decided to be firm rather than sympathetic. "Come on Greg, get up!" I shouted. He slumped back onto the ground. I leaned against the pillar, slid my back down until I too sat on the ground, and this time, allowed myself to cry.

I paused in the middle of a sob and looked through a watery blur. I thought I'd heard footsteps. Then, another sound like feet crunching on gravel, made me turn my head toward the parking lot a few yards away. Someone stood by the Volkswagen. I saw a small flicker of flame and then the burning glow of a lit cigarette. Could I be imagining things again? In the brief flare of the match, the face I'd seen was the "pirate" who'd disappeared. Was my mind so overwrought that everyone in the dark took on the same features? But if it really was him, why did he follow us? I didn't plan to wait around and find out if he disappeared again.

I found an energy and strength I didn't realize I still possessed. I tugged and heaved until I'd managed to get Greg up again. "Wake up. Get up!" I shouted.

"Wha..." At last, he allowed me to half-lead, half-drag him through the motel doors and down the long hallway to our room. In a panic, I couldn't find the key. I hastily dumped the contents of my purse onto the floor, and of course, it was the last thing to fall out.

I expected the door to open easily, since in the back of my mind I remembered that when we left, the door wouldn't shut all the way. Maybe the manager called in maintenance, though, as I found it firmly closed. It wouldn't open until I leaned against it and shoved hard with my shoulder.

I pushed Greg through the door, plopped him down on one of the beds, then quickly crossed the room back to the door and locked it. Now what? Who could I turn to for help? There wasn't any phone in the room, and I didn't want to venture out to find one. I doubted I could make my problems understood to the police anyway. Why hadn't they taught us what to say in an emergency, in my Spanish 101 class?

I decided to lie down on the other bed for a moment. My eyes focused sleepily on the window that wasn't a window and, though I struggled to keep them open, my eyes closed. I felt myself drift off to sleep.

I woke, shivering, and with a pounding headache. The room was chilly, but what woke me I think, was the sound of a door shutting. I was still half-asleep, when my eyes turned once again to the window. It was still dark outside and I could barely see the moon. But why did the window appear so high up in the wall and so small? Then I remembered, and sat up so fast, I got dizzy. I sat for a minute, reached out a hand to steady myself, and then walked over to the window. Then it dawned on my sleep-fogged brain...we were in a different room!

Why were we in a different room? How did we get there? We must have been drugged. What could we possibly have that someone wanted? Rich American tourists? Ha! They hadn't taken any of the rings off my fingers, or my necklace with its two tiny diamonds. And who were "they" anyway? I tried the door, though I knew it would be locked. Whoever put us in here certainly wouldn't let us leave.

Greg. He was already so sick, did they drug him too? I hurried over to his bed and sat down beside him. My heart pounded so loud I thought surely it would wake him, but he slept on. "Greg?" I whispered, and put my hand on his shoulder.

"Wha...?" he mumbled groggily.

"Greg, we've—" I froze at the sound of footsteps outside the door, then the rasp and click of a key in the lock.

The door opened with a jerk and banged against the wall. I sat up with my back against the headboard. The large woman manager stood there with two men—one of them the pirate, the other I'd seen talking to him on the boat. So, they *had* been following us. But why?

"What do you want?" I asked, trembling, but they ignored me. The pirate spoke in Spanish to the other man. But the other man cut him off, and motioned at me, saying that I understood Spanish.

The pirate picked up my purse from the floor and practically ripped it apart, looking through all the pockets. "Where is it?" he shouted angrily, taking a menacing step toward me.

I shrank back on the bed against the wall. "What? What are you looking for?"

"Maybe she doesn't have it," the other man said. "The girl was supposed to plant it on the other one." He gestured to Greg.

The pirate walked over to Greg then and slapped his face to wake him.

Greg came fully awake and sat up. "Run, Dee." He must have sensed we were in danger.

"No I'm not going to run." I forgot my fear. "Leave him alone! He's sick." I was ready to jump up and defend him, but the manager took my wrist in a vise-like grip.

"*Silencio!*" she commanded.

Greg tried to resist, but the pirate took full advantage. He twisted Greg's arm behind his back, who cried out in pain as I squirmed in the woman's grip. She squeezed my wrist so tight it went numb.

"What have you done with it? Where is it?" The pirate leaned down and shouted into Greg's face.

"I have no idea what you want, or why you're doing this," Greg said.

The pirate lost his temper, slapped Greg hard across his face, then thrust him roughly away. Greg fell back.

"Stop it! He told you we don't have what you're looking for!" I cried out, and got a sharp wrench of my arm from the manager for my efforts.

"Leave them," the pirate ordered the manager, and then the three of them left the room. As the lock clicked again, I stumbled to the door to listen. I didn't understand most of what they said, but one word did come through— *Pidalgo*.

Señor Pidalgo, the helpful Chamber of Commerce rep was involved too?

I hurried over to where Greg lay on the floor. I crouched down beside him and my tears overflowed. It wasn't only that I felt sorry for him, I realized then. I'd been fooling myself when I thought that I only wanted to be his friend. I'd always been attracted to him, but I didn't want to believe it was jealousy that caused my annoyance when he flirted with other women. I knew deep down I was also afraid of being hurt again. But Greg wasn't anything like Mark so I couldn't compare the two. Greg was sweet and smart—everything Mark wasn't.

Perhaps I would never have realized this if we hadn't been thrown together in these circumstances, but now I knew. I tenderly combed the still damp strands of hair off his forehead, and softly stroked his cheek. I raised my hand up to wipe the tears from my face and in the moon's light, I saw something dark and wet on my hand. There was a gash over his right eye.

Greg opened his eyes. "Why are you crying?" he whispered. He reached up and touched my cheek. When I didn't reply, he asked, "What's happening here, Dee? Do you know who those guys are?"

"They've been following us for a long time," I finally admitted. "I saw one of them on the flight to Los Angeles, and twice more after that. And then, the other man was dressed as a pirate on the boat. They seem to think we have something they want."

"Why didn't you tell me were followed?"

"Because I wasn't sure. I thought you would think I was paranoid and then you got so...so..."

"Sick?" He half-smiled sheepishly.

"Let me help you up," I said. I got him up off the floor and over to the bed, but then he accidentally pressed against my sore wrist and I pulled back and gasped in pain. Greg tried to keep me from falling as I teetered backward, but he was still unsteady on his feet, and we both toppled over onto the bed.

My arms were pinioned beneath him, my face only two inches from his. I felt as though I was in one of my romantic novels in which suddenly, "time stands still." *So it really does happen,* I thought. Greg stared into my eyes but didn't say anything. There was so much emotion on his face. I hoped it was all for me. I thought of that girlfriend back in Seattle, but since I seemed to have a bad habit of this—I kissed him.

I felt so shocked and embarrassed at what I'd done, I pulled away. But he drew me back toward him. I could feel his heart thumping wildly—or maybe it was mine. His arms tightened around me, and he kissed me. His hand cupped the back of my head, and his lips were warm and smooth. It felt so good.

"Greg..."

"Uh-huh..." he mumbled as he nibbled a trail to my neck.

"You have a girlfriend."

"No I don't." He continued to nibble.

"What?" I started to pull back again, but he reached up and pulled me to him. When we finally broke apart, I said, "We have to get out of here before they come back. Just as we started to rise, the key scraped in the lock. The door opened. I didn't recognize the two men at the door, but behind them, stood Ricardo. "Ricardo?" I mumbled. "Can't anyone be trusted?"

Ricardo motioned and I saw the pirate and the other man pulled past the door and out into the street. They were followed by the manager who appeared to be cursing in Spanish as her captor led her out.

Ricardo pulled out a badge. "I'm a detective, not an accountant."

Greg took it, looked it over and then handed it back, as Ricardo explained. "When you failed to show up at the cocktail lounge as usual the night before, we inquired about you at the Holiday Inn's front desk and learned that Brenda was sick and you went to Taxco. The more I got to know Brenda, the more I doubted that any of you were a part of this—you were dragged into a large diamond theft without your knowledge.

"Diamond...what?" I asked.

"We checked into your background. After I befriended you, I knew all of you weren't involved in the theft, but then you disappeared. We worried you were in harm's way."

"How did you find us?" I asked.

"If it wasn't for my cousin, Rosario, who rented the car to you, we may *not* have found you. When we asked the hotel manager to open Greg's room, and found it ransacked, we realized you were in danger. We'd already apprehended Laura Wilson who double-crossed her conspirators when she planted imitation diamonds in Greg's backpack and kept the actual jewels for herself."

Greg wiped a hand over his brow. "I assume Laura Wilson was the blonde at the airport back in Seattle, who claimed she lost her contact on the floor?"

"Yes. That's how she transferred the diamonds." The detective nodded and continued. "When the thieves searched Greg's room, they found only the fake diamonds. They assumed you kept the real ones on you and followed you to Taxco. You fell right into the foxes' den. They figured when they got the real diamonds, they could break them down to sell. You spoiled Pidalgo's plans once by not going to the silver mine—which he owns—and again when Greg got sick. He'd sent you to this motel which isn't actually in business anymore. His wife posed as the manager and had your bags searched. When they failed to find the diamonds in your luggage, we knew they would come back and kill you if we didn't get here first. We'll take a short statement and then the two of you are free to go."

I knew my knees shook by the time we gave our statements and the police left. Greg wound an arm over my shoulder and gave me a squeeze. His body felt warm and safe and I curled against him for a moment then looked up at him. "Let's get you to the hospital." I touched the cut on his head. "I think you might need stitches."

He took my hand and gave me a sweet kiss on my knuckles.

Later, Greg was released from the hospital with a big, square bandage on his forehead and looked...adorable. When we got outside, he motioned to me with this finger. "Come over here, will you Dee?" As I stood in front of him he said, "There's something I'd like to ask you. Well, it's kind of embarrassing, but...was I dreaming, or did you kiss me when we were in that place last night?"

I felt my cheeks flame. "How much do you remember?

"It's all a bit spotty, but I definitely remember a kiss. Did I kiss you back?"

"Yes," I admitted quietly. "You did."

"Good. Would you mind if I kissed you again? I'd like to know if it was as good as I remember." When I nodded, he pulled me close and his mouth captured mine. When we finally broke apart, he added, "I just wanted to make sure it was all real." He grinned.

"So, Greg, tell me about your girlfriend. First you said you had one, but then you said you didn't. So which is it?" I asked. I wanted to hear what he had to say now that we were out of danger.

"I don't have a girlfriend." He looked at me sheepishly. "I, uh, made her up."

"You made up a girlfriend?"

"Brenda was in on it. She knows how much I like you, but you only had eyes for Mark. She told me to be patient and suggested the fake girlfriend because then you wouldn't suspect my real motivation for coming on this trip. I wanted to spend time with you and see if it could work between the two of us. She told me not to give up hope and then when you kissed me before we left—"

"I gave you hope?" I interrupted.

"Brenda convinced me to go on the trip."

"You'll have to thank her for that. You got sick and almost killed."

"But I got to kiss you again." He smiled, and then frowned. "What about Mark?"

"Oh, I've moved on." I smiled to remind him of the words he'd spoken to me when I'd first kissed him for all the wrong reasons. "I realized how much time I wasted with Mark, when the right guy is here, in front of me."

Without Brenda's pushiness, I may never have seen the light. I'd finally figured it out—Greg was the only man for me.

When we got back to Seattle, we fell back into our old routines—and some new ones. I was in the middle of checking a passenger in, when I heard Brenda suck in a breath and say, "Uh-oh." A group of pilots stood around the ticket counter as usual chatting with her, but suddenly it got quiet, and when I looked up, I saw why. A few steps away from our counter, stood Greg. He walked up and grabbed my arm, then kissed me right there at the ticket counter for all the world to see.

"Greg!" I protested, but I smiled as I said it. "Everyone will see us." I heard people laugh, but for the first time in my life I didn't care.

"They just did." He kissed me again. "So, when do you wanna go away with me to Acapulco?"

"Make it Hawaii and you've got a date."

MARILYN CONNER MILES

HOLIDAY HEART

Chapter One

If she hadn't already given it up, Brenda would've smoked a cigarette to calm her nerves. She opened the sparkly red purse that matched her sparkly red dress, and dug out a pack of gum, then popped a piece into her mouth. At least maybe her throat wouldn't feel so dry.

She'd arrived at the Christmastime wedding for her friends Don and Marla in nervous anticipation of seeing *him* again. How would she handle it if there was another woman on his arm? Did he ever think about *her*? She'd searched the room for him as soon as she walked into the church and hesitated in the foyer outside the wide-open double doors. Someone touched her shoulder and she turned, startled.

Blake.

"Hello, Brenda," he said, and seemed to study her face for a moment before he offered his arm. "Ready to be seated?"

"Sure." She nodded, as her stomach fluttered. She'd hoped to appear aloof when she saw him, as though their breakup six years before was old news, but her uncooperative heart betrayed her. "You're one of the ushers?" was all she could think to say. Her throat seemed to close up, and for an instant she couldn't breathe, much less speak. She swallowed twice and then allowed her eyes to run lightly over him as she put a trembling, damp hand on the arm he offered.

As Blake escorted her to an evergreen bough-bedecked pew, she felt painfully aware of him next to her. His dark blue tuxedo appeared to be sewn onto his long, muscular frame. It molded to his broad shoulders and chest, tapered hips and long, slim, basketball player legs. She glanced up at his tanned face and his shorter than she remembered, thick, sun-streaked light brown hair. Did he get it cut for the wedding?

"I heard you moved to San Francisco. Do you like living there?" she asked when she'd recovered her voice. *Darn the man. Why did she always turn to a bundle of quivering nerves just at the sight of him?* Her stomach felt as though it bounced up and down like the mercury in an old thermometer. But his smile was her undoing.

"Yeah, I have a great job as an engineer for a huge company with lots of opportunities for advancement," he replied, eyes shining with enthusiasm.

She noted the enthusiasm with a pang. *Will he ever want to move back here?* she wondered.

"I have to return to my usher job now, but I'll see you later." He smiled. He'd taken her hand and still held it.

"Sure. Later."

"Yeah, right." He looked at her a moment longer. Was it her imagination, or was he reluctant to let go? But finally he released her hand. "Bye."

"Bye." She smiled and tried to act as casual as he appeared to be. With an effort, she refrained from watching him walk away and attempted to concentrate on the other guests. She looked ahead for any of their old friends, but didn't see anyone she knew. She could tell from the murmurs that the pews behind her filled up, but she refused to look back. She looked around the chapel instead at the festive evergreen swags with red bows, and the pots of red, white and pink poinsettias around the altar.

She'd felt so happy when she learned Don and Marla got engaged. They'd broken up nearly a year after her and Blake. Somehow, to hear they were back together and planned to make it permanent, made her wonder if maybe she and Blake could rekindle what they once had. She shook her head to rid herself of that foolish thought.

The music started, and the ushers walked up to the front of the church and stood with Don. Blake had caught Brenda's gaze and waved his fingers at her in acknowledgement as he passed by. She'd smiled briefly.

As the bride came down the aisle in a beautiful creamy lace dress, followed by her attendants in dark red velvet dresses, the guests stood. *Marla is so beautiful*, Brenda thought, and felt tears in her eyes, but if they were tears of happiness for her friends or sadness for herself, she didn't know. *It could have been Blake and me standing at the altar.* She saw some friends and forced herself to smile.

And then her smile died. There stood Blake's father and mother. Would his sister Amber be there too? She'd hoped to avoid all three of them. She felt sure they didn't want to see *her*.

When the ceremony ended and guests filed out to the lobby, Brenda stood, feeling awkward, and looked around hoping to find someone she could talk to. Attending a wedding by herself wasn't one of her favorite things to do, and especially at this time of the year when she felt even more alone. Her nerves surfaced again when Blake turned, and walked toward her.

"What are you doing these days?" he asked, his eyes scanning the area, as though making polite conversation. Maybe he hadn't come to the wedding alone. Maybe he was dating a woman his mother and sister approved of. "I heard that you work for an airline."

"Yes, I've been with WestAir for four years, now." Silence. *Why couldn't she think up something more interesting to say; something witty and clever that would make him want to stay at her side.?* She mentally scrolled through the databank of her memory and tried to call something up. *Ah...ah...yes, that's it!* "Well, I had quite an adventure in Acapulco a couple months ago." She smiled as she remembered the trip.

"Oh? What happened?" He seemed genuinely interested this time.

"A couple of my coworkers and I ended up involved in a diamond theft."

"What?" His eyes widened.

"Well, really, Deeann and Greg were more involved in it than me. You see, I knew they actually liked each other, but Dee was dating another pilot. He was a real piece of work, but of course, she didn't see it. I knew Greg would be great for her so when Dee broke up with Mark, I invited both of them to go to Acapulco with me...and the rest, as they say, is history." She'd said it all without taking a breath, hoping to keep his attention, worried he might be called away.

"You're leaving out something...the diamond theft?" he reminded her.

"Oh yeah, that." She was more interested in remembering the romantic parts of the story. "Well, a woman planted some fake diamonds on Greg when we landed in Los Angeles and the thieves thought he had the real ones, and then I got sick and went to the hospital—"

"What happened to *you*?" This time it sounded as though he was concerned as much as curious.

"Oh, just food poisoning, but—"

Blake interrupted her again. "How did *that* happen?"

"I thought you wanted to hear about the diamond theft."

"I *do*. Go ahead."

"Well, I missed most of it, being sick, but—"

"Hey Blake, get over here. The photographer wants to take the rest of the wedding party photos," Alan, one of the other groomsmen called.

Blake looked at Brenda and shrugged. "Sorry, I gotta go. I really wanted to hear what happened."

"No big deal. I know you have responsibilities as the best man."

"Good seeing you again, Brenda. See you later, okay?" He reached over and gave her a quick peck on the cheek. He still smelled like Cool Water. For a moment, she felt a wave of nostalgia, as she remembered their senior prom.

Brenda hoped she might get a chance to talk with Blake more before the evening ended. She waited around for awhile, but every time she looked up, he was busy—giving a toast and all the other best man duties. So, after the bride threw the bouquet, the groom threw her garter belt, the cake was cut and served and she'd talked at least once to all their old friends, she looked for him one last time. Blake stood with a glass in his hand, laughing with the other groomsmen. Time for her to leave, she realized as she finally gave up and walked out of the church to her car.

Chapter Two

At last, the early morning flights were gone and they had a few minutes to breathe before the next onslaught.

"Okay, Bren, spill it. How did it go? Was he there? Was he with someone?" Deeann peppered Brenda with questions from where she sat on a tall stool at the other end of the counter, a Christmas book in one hand. "Looks as though you were up late."

"Give me a few minutes, and I'll tell you, but first, I need to get some coffee. Want some?" Deeann shook her head and returned to her novel.

"You still read those love stories? I thought since you and Greg got together, you'd be too busy with your own romance."

Deeann looked up at her with sparkling eyes. "I'm addicted to them—especially the Christmas ones. I start reading them in November, though honestly I could read them 'year-round." She looked a little embarrassed at her confession, Brenda thought.

Deeann's hair wasn't mussed by wind and rain. Her makeup was neat and carefully applied and her uniform neatly pressed and wrinkle-free, with an angel on her lapel. *Greg must be flying in today*, Brenda thought, and then put a hand up to her face. She'd forgotten make-up! And she knew there must be bags under her eyes. When she grabbed a clean uniform jacket off the hanger before she flew out the door, she'd forgotten her name tag too. She'd hit the snooze button on her radio alarm clock three times before she felt awake enough to get up out of bed. Fortunately, it was the weekend and the station manager wouldn't be there to notice. She reached inside her purse, pulled out some lipstick and ran it over her lips.

There, maybe that might help.

Brenda headed for the coffee pot in the pilot's lounge behind the ticket counter, and grabbed her cup. But when she reached for the glass pot, she saw that it was nearly empty. It was the first stop the pilots made when they came in before their flights. Did she have time to brew more? The intercom buzzed, and she picked it up.

"Bren, there's someone out here asking for *you*," Deeann said over the line.

"Asking for me?"

"Yeah, by name."

"Thanks, I'll be right out." She glanced at the coffee pot and put it back on the burner. "Looks like I won't get that coffee after all," she muttered.

When she walked through the doorway and looked up, the pasted-on smile left her lips and became a real one. "Blake." She felt her heartbeat accelerate.

"Hey, Brenda."

She saw him look over to Deeann who darted a curious, quick glance back at him, before she returned to her novel.

"Uh, Dee, this is Blake. He was...is...an old...friend of mine. Blake, this is Deeann, the friend I went to Acapulco with."

They exchanged polite, 'nice-to-meet-yous' and then Blake looked around. "Slow day? I thought I'd have to stand in line to talk to you."

"Actually, we're in the eye of the storm right now. You missed the last onslaught. Any moment, the next wave will hit, and you won't even recognize sweet, shy me."

He snorted. "You? Shy?"

"Yes, me, but shortly my alter ego will emerge."

"This should be interesting. I think I'll just take a seat over there"—he tipped his head toward a group of bright orange-cushioned vinyl and chrome chairs near the huge, decorated Christmas tree—"and watch you in action." He walked off and sat down.

"Wait. What are you..." she tried to ask, but he grinned and pointed as a customer approached the counter, his arms full of bags and boxes to check.

Whenever there was a brief lull in passengers, she glanced up to see if Blake was still there. He reclined on the chair, his long legs stretched out, his arms draped over the chair on either side, a smile on his face. She quickly looked away.

She felt like a character in a play, acting out her part. Maybe she should charge admission. *Where's the popcorn?* she bit back the urge to yell at him. *What was he doing here anyway?* she wondered, struggling with an overstuffed seabag for a young military passenger.

"Can I help you with that ma'am?" the sailor asked eagerly, but she smiled and shook her head.

More passengers came and distracted Brenda from her thoughts of Blake for awhile. Finally, the last passenger checked in and the phone stopped ringing. Now she'd find out why Blake...she looked up. The chair was empty. She turned to Deeann to ask if she'd seen him leave.

"Don't you get a break?" Blake suddenly appeared in front of the counter with two festive peppermint mochas in his hands. He handed one to her, his fingers brushing against hers. She smiled as she took the coffee. He'd remembered how much she liked the Christmastime only treat. Then Blake handed the other coffee drink to Deeann, who smiled her thanks.

"Sometimes. Dee, I'm going on my break." When her friend nodded, Brenda told Blake, "Follow me." He hopped over the luggage scales and followed her to the back. "What are you doing here, Blake?" Maybe that didn't sound very friendly, but she needed to know.

"I had to hear the rest of the story, didn't I? Got any hot coffee?" He looked around the break room.

"Yes, we have a pot, but the pilots drank all of it. I'll make more, if you have time, though it isn't as tasty as the mochas you brought."

"Yeah, sure, that would be great. Thanks."

Brenda bustled about getting the coffee, still wondering why he was there. After they'd broken up six years ago she hadn't heard from him.

The com line buzzed on the phone. Brenda picked it up and listened. "Deeann again, needing reinforcements," she told Blake as she hung up the phone. "I need to get back to work. But the coffee's almost ready. Help yourself."

"No, I'll just go and get some at the coffee shop." He paused. "Hey, when do you get off work?"

"My shift ends at three o'clock," she said over her shoulder as she hurried out to the counter. She smiled at the passenger checking in and merely nodded when Blake called out to her as he walked away.

"See ya, Brenda."

"Yeah, sure," she mumbled.

****

Why did he ask her what time she got off work? Blake asked himself as he walked away. Now she'd expect him to call her. What was he doing, bringing her back into his life? He should stay away from her, see his friends and family and then go back to San Francisco the way he'd planned. If he had any sense, he'd do just that.

He'd wanted to feel indifferent. He'd wanted to think that she'd gone on with her life. The problem was, just seeing her again made him feel things he hadn't felt for any woman since their breakup. Maybe he wasn't as over her as he should be.

He knew he needed to see her again. He needed to see if what he'd remembered had been real love. And if it was, why had they broken up?

He must be crazy to think she still harbored any feelings for him.

****

As Brenda approached her apartment door, she heard the phone inside ring. Her left arm balanced a bulging bag of groceries and her right knee propped up another bag while her right arm supported it. She dropped the keychain from her teeth and held out her hand, cupped palm up, but missed. The keys dropped onto the damp grass and mud. The phone continued its insistent shrill.

"Oh shoot!" She put both bags down, picked up the key ring and shoved the key into the lock. She hurried inside, but half-way across the room, the ringing stopped. "Wouldn't you just know it?" she muttered. No red blinking light, so no message left on the answering machine. She sighed and walked back outside for the groceries. When she neared the phone, it rang again. She dropped the bags on the dining room table, and saw with disgust that one fell over and spilled half its contents.

"Hello," she said in irritation when she picked up the phone and watched a can of tuna roll off the table.

"Bad day, huh?" Blake's voice sympathized over the line.

"Sorry." Her heart sped up. *Why was he calling?* "Yes, it was."

"That's okay, I can be in a bad mood sometimes too."

"Yeah, I remember." There was a pause. She wondered what he was thinking. *Would he ever talk about their breakup?*

"When's your next day off?" he asked as though she hadn't spoken of anything else.

"Tomorrow. Why?"

"Do you have plans?"

"Well, I should clean my apartment, but if it's nice I might ride."

"Do you still have Carrot?"

Brenda smiled. He'd remembered. Carrot was her horse's name, but it used to be Blake's pet name for her. When he'd first seen her chestnut-colored horse, he'd looked from the horse to her. They had the same color hair. Carrot One and Carrot Two, he'd called them, but then he'd shortened it to just plain 'Carrot' for both of them.

"Yes. I keep her at my Uncle Jim's ranch in Cle Elum with his horses now. She's not alone, there are miles of trails to ride on and if I want to take someone riding with me, I can borrow one of his horses."

"Isn't there snow on the ground there by now?"

"Not yet. It's been an unusual year. They had some earlier, but none now.

"Who will you ride with if you go tomorrow?"

"No one. No one else works my crazy shift, except Deeann and she's afraid of horses."

"How'd you like to have a riding partner?"

"You?" She wondered if he heard the surprise in her voice.

"Do you mind?"

"No. I'm just surprised. I thought you'd be headed back to San Francisco.

"Not yet. I have a few days off."

Well…sure. Be sure to wear boots or shoes with hard heels."

"Yeah, I remember."

"Where are you staying? I'll pick you up."

"I have a rental car. Why don't I pick you up and we'll stop for breakfast?"

"Do you know where I live?" She'd moved at least twice in the years since he'd moved to San Francisco, and doubted any of their mutual friends knew since the wedding invitation arrived at her apartment with one of those yellow change-of-address stickers on it. She waited while he found a pen and something to write on, and then gave him brief directions. "See you in the morning, then."

She hung up the phone and as she unloaded the bags of groceries into the cupboards and refrigerator, she mulled over the events of the past twenty-four hours. Why had he called her now after all this time? What game was he playing? He was the one who broke up with *her* six years ago. *He* was the one who'd said their relationship "wasn't working."

Did Blake think he could just come waltzing back into her life and take up where he'd left off for a couple days, then leave her to go through the agony of trying to get over him a second time? She felt a familiar hollow pain in her chest.

I must have been crazy to think that he'd ever choose me over his family—especially his mom, she thought. *He'd made it clear back then, whose side he was on when he broke up with me.* Why would that change?

Well, she could spend the rest of the day and night thinking about what might have been; time to live in the present.

Chapter Three

A light fog shrouded the December morning sky when Blake picked Brenda up at her apartment. The air was crisp and cool, but not too cold. The rest of the neighborhood still appeared to be asleep, but she wanted to get an early start.

She looked him over from head to toe. She'd forgotten how good he looked in casual clothes—a T-shirt, jeans, and cowboy boots.

"Why did we have to get up at this disgusting hour? Don't you believe in sleeping in on your day off?" Blake grinned. He held a coffee mug in the hand not on the steering wheel.

"Morning's the best time to ride while the horses are fresh and feeling frisky. Once it warms up, like it has this week, they get lazy. Besides, you want to go for a long ride, don't you?"

"I don't know...I haven't been on a horse for a long time."

"You're not going to back out on me now, are you?"

"Oh, no..."

"It will be good for you to get out in that fresh air...and you can take a hot shower when you get back, and feel good as new."

"Where do you want to stop for breakfast?"

"Yeah, about that..."

"Hey, I'm hungry. Are you telling me you don't want to eat?"

"No. But I thought, rather than take the time to stop, I'd just bring something along and we could eat in the car as you drove." She reached behind her to the back seat and grabbed an insulated bag, then pulled out two large, foil-wrapped packages. "I have breakfast wraps and orange juice and that yummy candy cane-flavored coffee. How does that sound?"

"Great."

When they'd finished eating, Brenda felt a bit sleepy, staring out the window at the sun and the passing scenery. If she wasn't so excited about being with Blake again, she might have drifted off to sleep, lulled by the movement of the car and a full stomach.

But it seemed so unreal, going on a road trip again with Blake at the wheel like so many times in the past. There was a bubble of happiness in her chest and she knew she must have a huge smile on her face as well.

"How are your dad and Tim?" Blake broke the silence.

"Oh, Dad. He's still busy with work, but he's cut back some now that he has a steady girlfriend, Liz. Can you believe it?" Her smile faltered a little. "I don't see him much.

Blake looked over at her. "Do you like her?" He seemed hesitant to ask, but Brenda couldn't blame him.

"Yeah, I do," she said slowly.

Blake turned his attention back to the road, but Brenda didn't doubt that he wanted to know more. Instead he asked, "And your brother?"

"Oh, Tim likes her. He works with Dad now and goes over to his house a lot for dinner. Liz is a good cook, I hear.

"Well good for your dad."

She supposed she should reciprocate and ask about his family, but she couldn't make herself do it. She didn't want to bring up a sore subject and ruin the day, so she didn't ask.

****

"We're just about there. It'll be a great day for a ride," Brenda told Blake, as he glanced out the side window.

They'd turned off the highway onto the two-lane country road that led to the ranch. The sun peeped through the evergreen trees that grew thickly along the road. He opened the window a little and breathed deep to smell the sweet, fragrant odor of pine needles.

"You always wanted to live in the country," Blake said in remembrance, and turned his head slightly to smile at her.

"I still do." She sighed. "Maybe someday it will happen. Meanwhile, I'm lucky Uncle Jim has this place and lets me board Carrot here. Okay, you'll need to turn at that next unpaved road on the right," she told him.

They drove up the long, narrow gravel driveway, and Brenda directed him to stop the car in front of a large, two-story, ranch log home with a green corrugated metal roof. He got out of the car, and stretched. He looked around but didn't see any other vehicles. "Is your uncle here?"

"He doesn't seem to be. Maybe he's in town having breakfast, or visiting a neighbor down the road. I called him last night and asked if I could borrow Apache for my friend to ride and he said it was fine."

The ranch lay in a valley of acre upon acre of flat green pastures. Here and there were what was left of the original homesteads—ancient, crumbling, weather-beaten barns and other outbuildings, the sun bouncing bright rays off their newer, corrugated tin roofs. Mile after mile of often rusting, barbed wire fencing and tilting wooden posts, stretched across the land. In the distance, the rugged Cascade Mountain Range surrounded the valley.

As they drove in, Blake noticed that many farmyards were cluttered with rusting pieces of discarded farm machinery and automobiles, rotting lumber and useless plumbing fixtures. Ducks and chickens scratched in the mud. Children's bicycles and toys lay across the muddy brown lawns of tired, moss and vine-covered houses. Other farms were neater, with double-wide manufactured homes, encircled by well-kept flower gardens, birdbaths and wooden wishing wells on immaculately kept lawns.

These homes were interspersed with post and beam timber homes with their high-peaked roofs and floor-to-ceiling great rooms that belonged to the non-farm families. Burnt wood signs proudly displayed their owner's names. And farther down the valley, nearly hidden among the trees along the river, he saw the A-frame recreation cabins of their weekend families. He thought it was kind of sad to see the gradual change in the Teanaway Valley from farms and ranches to vacationland.

"There are the horses," Brenda said, breaking into his thoughts. She pointed to a half-dozen brown and red figures that grazed at the farthest end of a ten acre pasture.

"How do we catch them?"

"You'll see."

He watched as Brenda took a key on a string out of her pocket and fitted it into a large padlock on the thick old wooden barn door. She opened the door to reveal a low-ceilinged room. Long, thick pegs on the walls held various styles and sizes of western saddles draped with thick, wool horse blankets and pads. Smaller pegs above held halters with ropes, and leather bridles. Another wall supported a deep wooden, metal-lined grain bin, and Brenda walked purposefully toward it, grabbing a big metal scoop off the wall. She plunged the scoop into the grain bin, and then dumped the grain into two large coffee cans, and held them out to Blake. "Would you hold these?"

"Sure."

Brenda turned to another wall with shovels, post-hole diggers, and brooms lined up against it, and grabbed a large cowbell off a hook. "Follow me." She stepped outside, walked over to the pole fence, opened the gate, stepped through, and then held it open while he followed her, carefully looping the wire fastener back over the post. Then she shook the bell. "Now watch what happens."

At the first clap of the bell, the horses raised their heads as one, and turned to stare in the direction of the sound. When Brenda continued to ring it, they walked slowly to her, but soon their steps quickened. Then, the lead horse flung up his head, snaked it around and ran. The others galloped behind, as their tails flowed up and out behind them.

"Pour some grain into separate piles over there." Brenda pointed. She walked back through the gate to the barn again and came back out with halters and lead ropes attached to them.

"Doesn't your uncle ever feed them?"

"Yes, of course, but they *love* grain." Here, I need your help again." She handed him a halter and rope behind her back. "Don't let them see this. Now walk up to that bay horse with the star on his forehead. That's Apache. Pretend you have something else for him and then slip the rope around his neck."

After the horses were caught and tied to the hitching post, Brenda brought out brushes, handed one to him, and reminded him to brush the way Apache's hair grew. He coughed at the dust. He saw Brenda look over and grin as he fed the horse a carrot. She nodded in approval. "Smart move. Now you're his buddy."

****

"The horses are eager at first, when they start out—feeling their oats," Brenda said, as she smiled at Blake. She was surprised to see he hadn't forgotten a thing about riding, and looked like a regular horseman.

The horses seemed to be trying to outdo each other in a trotting race up the trail—no easy feat since the trails went mostly uphill. At the top, where the trail intersected with an abandoned logging road, Brenda reined Carrot in.

"We shouldn't have let them do that. They need to warm up first like any athlete," she told Blake, but she couldn't help smiling. The crisp mountain air was still brisk and invigorating and the horses' breath puffed out in the cold misty air.

"Hey, this is great." Blake looked out at the view.

"You get a much better view of nature from the back of a horse, than you do in a car. And, the air smells better."

There was nothing like riding up into the mountains on horseback. Trail-riding calmed her and gave her a peaceful feeling. She loved to be up above the tree line in the fresh air, away from the deafening noise of the city—and the airport. The tall trees made a canopy across the trail, but sometimes when she looked up she could see patches of blue sky.

"This reminds me of flying," Blake said. "I got my pilot's license a couple years ago. You can see so much more from the air too."

"The trail we're on goes past what's left of an old log cabin. It's really cool. It must be over a hundred years old. I doubt that you could see it from the air—it's pretty well-hidden—but we're heading for Bible Rock. It has a great view of the whole valley. It's at the very top of this mountain and from the distance it looks like an open book. You might feel as though we are in the clouds then." She smiled.

Blake peered up the trail. "How long will it take to get there?"

"Only about two hours."

"Two hours...*up*?"

She laughed. "Yes, and two hours back down. Is that too much for you?"

"No..." he answered, but she could hear the hesitation in his voice. Brenda just smiled. As the sun rose overhead, she felt too warm—or maybe it was the sight of Blake in his cream-colored fisherman's sweater, and worn jeans, better-looking than any man had a right to be, that warmed her. At first, she'd felt glad she'd worn her sheepskin-lined denim jacket, but now she felt a need to peel off at least one layer of clothing.

"Blake, stop for a minute. I want to take off my jacket." She pulled back on the reins and Carrot stopped, and then stretched her long neck down to grab a grass snack while she could. Brenda reached around, placed her folded jacket behind the saddle's seat and tied it in two places with the attached leather strings. She looked up, and saw that Blake struggled to do the same with his sweater, but Apache wouldn't cooperate. He pranced and pulled on the reins, trying to get to the grass.

"Hey, whoa horse!" He grabbed at the reins to hold his mount's head up.

"Here, give me the reins and I'll hold him for you," Brenda offered, and reached out her arm. "Apache's a good riding horse, but Uncle Jim doesn't spend much time working with him. He doesn't have very good manners."

"Nah, I can do it. I'll just get off and let him graze like Carrot, and then I can use both hands." Blake dismounted, and grabbed for his sweater. Before he could pull it off the dancing horse, the sweater fell to the ground. Startled, the horse jumped forward smack into Carrot, who squealed, laid her ears back against her skull and kicked out. Apache leaped sideways to avoid the vicious thrust of Carrot's hoof, but Blake, caught in the middle of them, didn't. He fell to the ground, and grasped his thigh with both hands.

Brenda saw a bright splotch of blood spread under his fingers.

"Blake!" she cried, horrified, as he sank slowly to the ground. She ran over to him. His jeans were torn where the horse's shod hoof landed. She didn't know much about first aid, except that she should try to stop the bleeding, and that the wound should be cleaned. She grabbed her canteen and jacket from Carrot's saddle, thankful that her horse calmed down after her annoyance with Apache. She cropped at the grass and allowed Brenda to walk up to her.

Brenda found a large, clean bandanna in her jacket pocket and soaked it with water from the canteen. "Blake, your jeans are already torn here, but I have to tear them some more to get to your wound, okay?"

"Yeah, go ahead. Do what you have to do."

Brenda dabbed at Blake's wound after she'd applied pressure long enough to stop the flow of blood. Her heart raced and she had to fight a woozy feeling. The sight of blood always made her feel faint, but she needed to keep going. She pulled her jacket from the saddle and laid it under his head for a pillow, then grabbed his sweater off the ground where it landed, and laid it over him.

He'd closed his eyes briefly, but opened them again. "How is it?" he asked with a grimace.

"I got the mud cleaned off and it's not bleeding much right now, but I think you'll need stitches. You can't ride even if I *could* catch Apache, and you can't walk, so I'll need to go back to the ranch and get some help. Will you be okay here by yourself?"

"Yeah, I'll be all right. What will you do with Apache?"

"I think he'll follow Carrot. I'd better get going. Are you sure you'll be okay here alone?" she asked anxiously. He looked so pale.

"I forgot how hard horses can kick." He gave her a wan smile and nodded.

"I put the canteen right next to your hand in case you get thirsty. Anything else I can do for you before I go?"

"How about a kiss?" A smile quirked at the corners of his mouth, and then immediately turned to a wince.

"You must not feel too bad if that's all you want." She leaned over to give him a quick peck on his lips, but his hand laced around her neck and he pulled her down. His lips were arm and still tasted of candy cane coffee. She wanted the kiss to go on forever. When he released his grip on her, she pulled back, and stood up, stunned for a moment.

"I feel better now. That helped." His eyes were closed, but a slight smile played on his lips.

Brenda backed away. No, this couldn't happen. He'd broken up with her. Nothing had changed. He'd leave again in a few days. "I'll be back as quick as I can," she said, turned and hurried over to Carrot.

She thrust her foot into the stirrup and hopped up into the saddle on Carrot's back. "Come on girl, you need to fly," she urged the horse, and turned her toward the trail, with one last look at Blake.

Instead of heading back down the trail they'd just ridden up, she took a shortcut that should get her back to the ranch faster. Sure enough, Apache, ears pricked forward, came whinnying after them at a full gallop, stirrups flapping, as fast as the horse could run downhill through the trees and brush, trying to avoid his trailing reins.

Brenda felt relieved to see her uncle's old Chevy pickup parked in front of the cabin. When she called out, "Uncle Jim," he appeared in the doorway.

He reached out to grab the reins of the riderless horse. "Whoa, Apache. What's wrong, Brenda?

After she'd caught her breath, she explained and ended with, "It's all my fault. I should have let him ride Carrot, but she can be pretty spirited. I thought Apache would be safe for Blake. I had no idea Carrot would kick him."

"No time for regrets. Put the horses away and I'll get an old mattress to put in the back of the truck. We can get pretty close to him on one of those old logging roads."

Brenda unsaddled the horses, pulled their bridles off and turned them into the corral by the barn. She knew she should walk and cool them and rub them down after their mad dash, but Blake needed her. "Sorry guys." She ran back to the cabin and hopped into the pickup.

Blake's eyes were closed when they reached him, but he must have heard them and sat up part-way.

"I brought help. Blake, this is my Uncle Jim. Thank goodness he was home. How are you doing?" Brenda asked in a rush as she dropped down beside him.

"Not too bad. A bit embarrassed to be so helpless, though. Nice to meet you, sir," he replied and then sucked in a breath as he moved an inch.

"Don't worry about that. We brought my truck, but the road only got us so far. I'm afraid you'll have to walk a bit—with our help, of course. Let's see if we can get you up on your feet without making things worse."

Brenda's uncle helped her get Blake to his feet. "I think I can walk now, if I can just hold onto you a little, Brenda," Blake told them. She nodded and moved closer to him. He put his arm around her shoulders, and she felt his big, warm body against hers. It felt all too familiar. She sighed.

"Am I too heavy for you?" Blake asked. "I might be able to make it on my own…"

"Oh no. You're fine. I was just…thinking, that's all. The truck's just a bit farther."

They were able to get him to the truck and onto the mattress in the pickup bed. Brenda sat in the back with his head in her lap and tried to cushion him from the bumpy, rutted, old dirt road, and shield him from the dust that flew up around them, and into their eyes and mouths.

When they reached the cabin, Brenda asked Blake, "Can you semi-recline in the back seat of the car while I drive you to the ER?"

"Sure." He frowned. "This wasn't how I'd planned for this day to work out at all," he mumbled, then turned and hobbled toward the car.

Chapter Four

The drive was mostly silent. Blake lay partially propped up against the back seat. Every time Brenda took her eyes off the road to glance back at him, his eyes were closed. He had to be in terrible pain. She'd been kicked, though not this bad, and she knew how much it hurt.

Blake cracked an eye. "It's just a cut." But she saw blood seeping through the gauze she'd found in her uncle's first aid kit.

When she pulled up to the emergency entrance of the hospital, Brenda hopped out of the car and ran in through the automatic double glass doors. "I need a wheelchair!" she shouted out to the woman behind the reception desk. A nurse, who stood behind the desk as well, found a chair and followed Brenda out to the car. The two of them helped Blake into the chair. Brenda parked the car and ran back inside, but didn't see him in the waiting room, so she walked up to the reception desk. "I'm the one who needed the wheelchair. Do you know if the nurse took him back there?" She pointed to the double doors that led back to the triage area.

"I think so. What is his name?"

"Blake Preston."

The receptionist nodded.

"Can I go back there and be with him?"

"Are you a relative?"

"No, but—" Worry clenched her gut.

"Then I'm sorry, you'll have to wait out here."

"Sharon, that's okay, he's asking for her." The nurse who'd wheeled him in, stood in the doorway, and beckoned for Brenda to follow her."

Blake lay on top of a railed bed, his eyes closed, while a nurse took his blood pressure. He wore a blue hospital gown. The bed seemed small for his large frame.

Brenda waited until the nurse finished checking his vitals to ask him, "How do you feel?"

"Honestly? It hurts like hell. My thigh feels as though it's on fire."

Brenda turned to the nurse. "Can't you give him something for it?"

"I'm sorry, the doctor needs to see him first and then we can give him something for the pain." The nurse patted Blake's shoulder, told them the doctor would be in shortly, and left the room.

"I'm so sorry this happened to you. You'll probably never want to go riding or have anything to do with horses again." Brenda sighed and looked down, tears forming in her eyes. For the first time that day, now that Blake was in capable hands, and the adrenaline that kicked in had receded, she let herself cry.

"Hey, don't cry." He gestured for her to sit on the side of the bed. "It's not your fault. Accidents happen. I'll just have to be more careful around horses in the future and get out of the way faster when they kick at each other. Actually, I was having a great time. Look on the bright side:

it was such a short ride I didn't have a chance to get saddle sore," he said and then smiled at her through clenched teeth.

She smiled back through her tears, wiped them away with the back of her hand and sniffed. "You've always known how to cheer me up. You're the one injured, I should try to make *you* smile."

"You always make me smile."

Brenda felt relieved when they didn't have to wait too long for the doctor to come in. But when he began his exam, poking and prodding at the wound to assess the damage, the look on Blake's face made her reach for his hand. He turned his head to look at her and his mouth tugged up in a brief smile—well, maybe a grimace—that tugged at her heart.

"Yes, it definitely needs stitches," the doctor told them. "But you're lucky. I got a look at the x-rays and it just missed the bone, so your leg's not broken. I'll have the nurse come in and give you some pain meds and a shot to numb the area before I stitch it up. We'll have you feeling better soon," he said and walked out of the room.

Not soon enough, Brenda thought. It was hard to see Blake in such pain. She squeezed his hand in sympathy.

When the nurse came back in, she handed Blake a pill and a small paper cup of water, and then looked at Brenda. "The doctor will be back in shortly to stitch up Mr. Preston's wound, so if you don't want to stay, Mrs. Preston, you could go right down the hall to the waiting room, and I'll let you know when he's done."

Brenda was sure her mouth gaped open. "Uhhh..."

"You'll stay, won't you Brenda?" Blake seemed to plead. He knew her aversion to the sight of blood. He'd always put the Band-Aids on her when she had cuts. He'd had to put them on himself too, and told her to sit down when she felt woozy. She knew that he realized how much he was asking of her.

"Yes, of course." She swallowed, and her hands felt clammy.

But Brenda surprised herself by handling the procedure better than she thought. She looked away when the doctor first put the needle in, but when she saw Blake's reaction, she again reached for his hand and held it tight. And when he started to look down, she tugged on his hand to get his attention.

"So, what made you decide to finally get a pilot's license? You talked about it for years." It did the trick and as he explained. Brenda listened and felt she made the appropriate responses to keep him talking, but she couldn't help but wonder who she hoped to distract—Blake or herself?

Brenda brought the car up to the ER entrance and then got out to help Blake into it. Then she drove them to the drive-through pharmacy window to get the prescribed pain medication filled.

"Where now?" she asked him, though she knew the obvious answer.

"You can take me back to your place and I'll drive back to my parents' house from there."

"Blake, you can't drive when you're taking pain medication. I'll just take you there and find a way home." She sighed. If she was lucky, his parents were still at work. She glanced at her watch. It was much later than she'd thought. ER visits always took a long time.

"Okay. I'm sure I can find someone to drive you back to your place," he said drowsily, the pain pills obviously doing their job.

When they reached his parents' dark brown, split-level home in an older sub-division, a car sat in the driveway.

"Looks as though someone is here," Brenda said.

Blake barely opened his eyes and squinted. "Oh, it must be Amber."

Great, Brenda thought. *I know what his sister thinks of me.* But she tamped down her feelings of unease, and got on with the chore of getting Blake out of the car and into his parents' house.

Before they got half way up the sidewalk to the house, Amber came out with an anxious look on her face.

"What happened?" She turned to Brenda with a frown and took Blake's other arm. "*I'll* help him now," she said in a sharp tone of voice as though to imply that Brenda was no longer needed—or wanted—there.

"I've got him," Brenda replied, taking a firmer hold on his arm.

Blake looked back and forth between them, and then said calmly, "Could you get the door Amber? I'll tell you what happened later." When his sister frowned but nodded, he added, "Oh, and Brenda needs a ride home. You'll take her, won't you?" Brenda knew if she wasn't so busy watching where she walked, she would see an even bigger frown on Amber's face—or worse.

"Are you staying in the guest room?" she asked him once they were inside the house. When he nodded, she continued to walk with him down a long hallway. When she got him settled on the bed, his eyelids were at half-mast. She heard a noise and looked up to see Amber in the doorway.

"Are you ready to go home?" the younger woman asker her in an unfriendly tone. It was obvious that she would only do it because Blake asked her to, but Brenda knew Amber must be struggling to remain civil to her.

"Okay. I just want to say goodbye."

"It looks like he's asleep. Let's go." Amber turned and walked away.

But as Brenda turned away to leave the room, a hand reached out and grabbed her arm. "Thanksss for helping me..." Blake took her hand, and with a groan pulled her down against him. He lifted his head off the pillow a few inches and without warning closed the distance between them and kissed her. Without thinking about it, she kissed him back.

"I have to go. Amber is waiting to give me a ride home." She wanted to stay with him, but didn't want to anger Amber.

"You'll come back and visit me, see how I'm doing, won't you?" He kept a hold of her hand.

"I'll try."

"Please, Brenda..."

"Okay," she conceded. With any luck, Amber wouldn't be there then.

"Promise?" he whispered.

She sensed he wouldn't let go of her until she did. "Cross my heart," she said and made the sign over her heart.

Although she'd rather be anywhere else but in a small car with Blake's sister, Brenda reluctantly folded her body into the passenger seat of Amber's sub-compact. She reached around and pulled the shoulder harness over and clicked it into place, then gave the other woman the directions to her apartment complex.

They rode in silence for awhile until Amber demanded in an accusatory tone of voice, "What happened to him? Mom said he left the house early this morning before she got up."

"He went riding with me and got kicked by my horse," Brenda answered with averted eyes as she looked out the passenger side window. "He needed to have stitches, but I cleaned the wound pretty well and the ER doctor said there shouldn't be an infection. He should be okay..." she trailed off.

"Hmmph," Amber grunted. "I don't know why he's spending time with you," she muttered under her breath, but loud enough so that Brenda clearly heard every word. "When you broke up with him, you broke his heart!"

What?

She'd meant to say as little as possible to Blake's sister, but Amber had it all wrong. Blake had broken up with *her*. She turned to look at Blake's sister. "Listen Amber… " Brenda started to tell the other woman the truth, but decided she needed to talk to Blake about it first. "I know you don't approve of me, but Blake's an adult and he can do what he wants...and just so you know, I didn't initiate this contact with him. I was at Don and Marla's wedding—"

"I saw you there," the other woman said sulkily.

"—and the next day he came to see *me* at my job."

When Amber opened her mouth to interrupt again, Brenda held up her hand and continued with barely a hesitation.

"He called me that night too—not that it's really any of your concern." She turned away and looked out the window again. Why was it taking so long to get to her place? Just then, she saw the apartment complex. "Okay, you can let me off here. I-I need to check my mailbox," she said, scrambling for a reason to get out of the car. Fortunately, Blake's sister didn't say another word, probably just as eager to be rid of *her*. She stopped the car, waited for Brenda to get out, and then drove off without a goodbye.

****

Blake lay on the guest room bed, waiting for the time to pass before he heard the slam of the door that would announce the arrival of, he assumed, his angry sister. Either it came sooner than he'd expected, or he'd dozed off. If so, the slam of the door and the hurried footsteps coming down the hall woke him. And then she stood there in the doorway, a frown on her face, her hair mussed. She threw her large handbag on the bed and then she plopped herself down next to it.

"Oomph." He gritted his teeth, as much from the pain of the bounced mattress as from the lecture he felt sure would follow.

"Blake, what in the world are you doing?"

"Lying here, trying to forget the pain," he answered and closed his eyes, though he knew full well what she meant.

"I'm not trying to interfere, you know. I just remember what it was like before and I'm trying to save you from getting hurt—again."

"That was six years ago, Amber," he said in a quiet voice.

"She's bad news for you, brother. Last time she hurt your heart and this time your leg!" Her loud, excited voice hurt his head. Pain medicine always gave him a headache. "Maybe you have, but *I* haven't forgotten that she broke up with you."

No, he hadn't forgotten, and he felt a lot of guilt about it. After he broke up with Brenda, Amber assumed that *she* broke up with *him*. His sister thought Brenda didn't want anything to do with his family. And he'd never corrected that assumption. All this time, he'd let her and the rest of his family believe that it was true. Time to come clean and tell them the truth—*he* was the one who walked out on Brenda.

Why *did* he leave her?

Chapter Five

Brenda put her key in the lock and opened the door of her apartment, then flopped down into her glider rocker. She kicked off her shoes, put her feet up on the ottoman and heaved a sigh. She should think about throwing something together for dinner, but she didn't feel hungry. She felt truly alone for the first time in a long time—since she and Blake broke up.

Sure she'd had her fantasy of them getting back together. Foolishly, after they'd broken up, she waited by the phone in case Blake called her to say he'd made a terrible mistake. But he never called. And earlier that day, she'd let herself get lost in the joy of the time she spent riding with him. It felt so good to be with Blake again. But after she'd spent just a short time with Amber, she realized it would never happen. She felt sure Blake's sister would go back to their parents' house and remind him of the reason he broke up with Brenda in the first place.

In her heart, Brenda knew she was to blame for the breakup. She'd found so many convenient excuses not to spend time with Blake's family. It wasn't that she didn't *like* his family. They joked and had a good time, and were always polite with her, as though trying to make her feel welcome. And his mother seemed like a nice woman. But Brenda felt *smothered* by her. She'd call or Amber would call on her behalf and invite Brenda over to the family home for "girl only" get-togethers with her and Amber and Blake's aunts and female cousins.

After her own mother left, Brenda hadn't wanted to leave the house for even a minute. She was afraid that her mother might come back and she'd miss her. She'd kicked and screamed when her father forced her to go to school. Her dad must have been desperate for a replacement mother for his children, when he'd brought home Dana, a woman his friends set him up with.

But Dana wasn't interested in kids; only their father. Oh sure, at first she'd cozied up to them, and Brenda, desperate for a mother again, believed her. She'd felt crushed when her dad suddenly stopped seeing the woman. But she'd overheard him talking to a friend on the phone after that. "Yeah, that's over. She didn't like my kids."

Brenda knew that she'd spent most of her life withdrawing from anything that might cause her hurt. She'd held back, afraid of rejection—especially from women who'd tried to mother her. And with Blake's mother, she'd withdrawn just as she always did when faced with the risk of rejection.

For years after that, it had been just the three of them—her dad, Tim and her. As an adult she avoided the holidays like the plague. She attended required company parties but avoided any attempts from friends or coworkers to include her in theirs. She told herself family holidays weren't really the warm and fuzzy time they were cracked up to be. She had to tell herself that to keep from yearning for something she couldn't have.

And then she'd risked her heart—with Blake. And look how that turned out. But now, even her dad had someone in his life and didn't need her. And Deeann, her one close friend, had Greg in her life and less time to spend with Brenda.

Sure, she was popular with the pilots at work, and they always hung around the ticket counter and talked to her, but they were more acquaintances than true friends. She felt as though she'd lost everyone she had ever been close to, beginning with the mother who abandoned her years before.

Would she ever be important enough, *loved* enough?

When Brenda nervously called Blake's cell phone the next morning to check on him, he answered sleepily—still on pain pills, she assumed.

"Can you come over?" he asked.

"I'm at work, so I can come over afterward… around three-thirty?"

"Great…I'll be here…" he seemed about to doze off and soon she heard a dial tone.

"How's he doing?" Deeann asked as she slung a bag onto the belt that carried it downstairs to the baggage handlers. "Oomph! That's a heavy one." She slapped her hands together to get rid of the dirt.

"I told him I'd go over there after work. No one is there now, but I don't know about later. He dozed off on the phone before I could ask," she answered with a frown.

The rest of the day flew by until the last hour before her shift ended, and all she could think about was, *What if when I go over to see Blake, his mother is home?* Bad enough dealing with Amber unexpectedly the day before, but to see his mother again…what could she say? Despite Deeann's reassurance, she didn't know how his mother would react to seeing her again. Brenda felt certain Mrs. Preston would not want her in the house.

When Brenda arrived at the Preston's house, rather than ring the doorbell, she called Blake from the car on her cell phone.

"Hello?" He sounded more awake this time.

"I'm here," she told him.

"Come on in. The door isn't locked."

"Is anyone home with you?" She'd looked when she first arrived but didn't see a car in the driveway or parked on the street in front of the house.

"No, just me," Blake answered.

"I'll be right there," she said, and ended the call. She felt a little weird walking into the house, but Blake called out to her and she followed the sound of his voice to the family room where he lounged on a plum-colored vinyl sofa. He held a remote in one hand and she could hear voices coming from a television. His leg was propped up on a coffee table next to a tray of empty dishes and glasses. She could smell the pungent aroma of the decorated Christmas tree in the corner—or maybe it came from the two lit red and green candles on the mantel of the fireplace where several plush red stockings hung.

"Thanks for coming. Sit down." Blake patted the sofa next to him.

"Before I sit down, can I get you anything?" Brenda asked as she leaned over and dropped her purse on the floor.

"Yes, a refill on this would be nice." He held up a glass."

"What are you drinking?" she asked, and took the glass from his hand.

"Some kind of cola." There's a big bottle in the fridge door, if you don't mind getting it."

Brenda shook her head and walked back to the kitchen. Though she was quite familiar with the house, she hadn't been there in several years. Nothing much seemed to have changed, except more photos and magnets added to the refrigerator door. It felt awkward to roam through the house.

When she got back to the family room with Blake's glass of soda, and sat down on the sofa, he said, "It's a little chilly in here, don't you think? Mom turns the heat down during the day when everyone is gone. Guess she forgot I'm here."

"Where's the thermostat? Do you want me to turn it up?" She looked around.

"No, Mom would probably have a fit. She already complained about the sky-high utility bills a couple nights ago. You know what would really help? Scoot closer and I'll cover both of us with this throw.

Brenda complied. It *did feel* a little chilly. She didn't want to get too close and risk bumping his injured leg, so she left several inches between them.

Blake shivered. "This little Christmas throw isn't big enough. You'll have to scoot closer."

Brenda frowned. "Your leg..." she began, but Blake beckoned her closer. She moved gingerly, trying not to touch him, but he put his arm around her and covered them with the throw.

"There, isn't that better? Warm enough?" Blake asked with a smile.

Brenda nodded, and tried to hold herself stiffly away from him, but the warmth from his body felt so good. She found herself thinking back to times they'd curled up together on this sofa and "watched" TV." She knew she wanted to ask him something, but couldn't remember. Oh, yeah. "Did Amber talk to you when she got home?"

"Yeah, she's still talking to me."

"You know what I mean...about me."

"We might have talked about you. I don't remember. These drugs you know..." he gestured to the prescription bottle on the coffee table.

"Blake, what did you tell—" but Blake's eyes closed and she decided not to pursue it. She'd talk to him about it later. Brenda pulled a red and green afghan off the arm of the couch and covered them. She struggled to stay awake, but it had been a busy day at work and she hadn't slept well the night before thinking about Blake, and his warm arm around her felt comforting....

Brenda struggled to come awake from a dream. She heard voices, but if they were from the dream or real, she didn't know. When her eyes popped open, she thought, *This isn't my bed. Where am I?* Then she looked up.

There stood Mrs. Preston and Amber.

Chapter Six

Darn. Just what she'd been afraid of. Brenda snuck a quick glance over at Blake—fast asleep—before she tossed the afghan aside and sat up. She felt like a high school kid caught fooling around after school with her boyfriend while his parents were at work.

"Amber, M-Mrs. Preston. Hello," she stammered. Amber continued to frown, then abruptly turned on her heel and walked out of the room. Would Mrs. Preston do the same—or worse?

But to her great surprise, Blake's mother smiled. "Hello, Brenda. Thank you for coming over to help Blake while everyone else is at work. Can you stay for dinner? We're just having soup and sandwiches. It's easier for Blake right now if he doesn't have to sit too much and bend that leg. He's been eating here at the coffee table."

Brenda didn't know what to say. She wanted to get in her car and leave. What excuse could she give? Out of the corner of her eye, she saw Blake stir, and suddenly his hand came out from under the throw and clasped her arm. "Please stay."

"I...uh..." This would be the time to come up with an excuse just as she'd always done in the past when Mrs. Preston asked her to have a meal with them. "I...okay, that would be nice. Th-thank you. Um...do you need some help?"

It seemed as though the smile on Blake's mother's face grew wider. "Oh no, dear. It won't take but a few minutes. I've had the soup simmering in the Crockpot all day. It's Blake's favorite, minestrone. I don't get to cook for him very often. I wouldn't wish him this injury, but at least he's spending a little more time with us than he'd planned, I think."

When his mother left the room, Blake said, "Thanks," and patted her hand. "Don't worry, it will just be us. Amber probably went home and Dad likes to eat at a table with a tablecloth. And of course, Mom will eat with him."

Brenda nodded, but she was still in shock. Why did his mother seem to accept her there? Did Blake warn her that Brenda might be there when she got home from work? But Mrs. Preston seemed almost *happy* to see her.

Brenda continued to visit Blake after work for the rest of the week, and every evening when his mother got home, she asked Brenda to stay for dinner, and Brenda accepted. It was hard to resist the wonderful smells that came from the kitchen.

By the end of the week, Blake was able to eat dinner at the dining room table, so she sat with him and his parents, but by then she felt more comfortable with them. Blake's dad had always been nice to her and still was. Amber seemed to be staying away and for that Brenda felt grateful.

Brenda felt sure Blake's sister wouldn't be as forgiving as her mother.

Her only real problem seemed to be Blake himself. Sometimes when she knocked, then walked in the front door, he greeted her with a smile, but at other times, he frowned and appeared grumpy. She supposed he felt antsy, unable to get around much, and watching the television all day must get old. Still, she thought he'd welcome the company and the distraction.

One evening, when his mother got home, Brenda felt so fed up with his attitude, she decided she'd leave and planned to say no when his mom asked her to stay for dinner. She stood up when she heard the automatic garage door open and saw the flash of headlights from Mrs. Preston's car as she pulled into the driveway.

"Your mom's home, Blake. You don't seem to be up for company tonight, so I think I'll go home. Maybe you'll feel better tomorrow." She reached for her coat and purse.

"You'll hurt Mom's feelings if you don't stay for dinner," Blake reminded her.

Yes, there was that. But how could she stay when he didn't seem to want her there? Before she could respond, Mrs. Preston walked into the house and back to the family room.

"Brenda, I made *your* favorite meal tonight. I sure hope you can stay for dinner," she said with a huge grin.

Oh no, Brenda groaned inwardly. *How can I turn that down?* She couldn't. "That must be the heavenly smells I've noticed since I got here. Of course I'll stay. You are so kind, Mrs. Preston. How did you know?"

"I asked Blake," the other woman replied with a smile.

Brenda turned and looked at Blake, but he stared intently at something on the TV screen. Brenda sighed. "Well, at least let me set the table," she said and followed Blake's mother into the kitchen.

"Brenda, I'm glad you stayed. I've wanted to talk to you—alone," Blake's mother said in a soft voice, when the dark wood swinging saloon-style louvered doors closed behind them.

Oh-oh. Brenda tensed.

"I think I know the reason you broke up with Blake. It was because of me."

What? There it was again. Another member of his family saying that she broke up with him. "Oh, uh, no..." Brenda felt compelled for some reason to reassure Blake's mother.

"I interfered and I know now that I made you uncomfortable."

"You were just being kind," Brenda acknowledged. "You've always been nothing but kind to me."

"Well, I did something wrong. I guess I pushed too hard to make you feel accepted and part of our family." Mrs. Preston smiled tentatively. "You see, Blake told me that your mother left and that you grew up with just your father and brother, and no one—not even a grandmother or aunt—to mother you."

The confession from Blake's mother was so different from the lecture she'd expected to get, Brenda felt stunned and momentarily at a loss for words.

"Do you think you can ever forgive me?" the older woman asked her sadly.

"Forgive *you*? I was the one who rejected your kindness. *I'm* the one who needs to ask for forgiveness," Brenda answered, surprised yet again. She felt tears come to her eyes, and when Mrs. Preston reached out to her with open arms, Brenda felt no qualms about accepting the comfort and forgiveness. *She needed to have a talk with Blake.*

After the hug, they just smiled at each other for a few moments through their tears until Blake's mother stepped back and said, "Now let's get that dinner served."

"Do you like to fly?" Blake asked her one day as she sat with him, idly flipping through the *Aviation News* magazine on his bed.

"Sure. Of course."

"I mean, in a small plane. Not a jet."

"I guess so. I've only gone up once, in a seaplane to the San Juan Islands.

"Great. How about if I pick you up at 8:00 tomorrow morning?"

"What? You're kidding, I hope. You're not in any shape to fly."

"Sure I am."

"Are you sure?" Brenda frowned at him. She hadn't gone in with him when she'd given him a ride to his doctor's appointment for the follow-up after his ER visit. "Did your doctor say it's okay?"

"He said it's up to me."

Brenda wondered about the hesitation in his answer, but he should know whether he could fly. "Well, okay," she agreed hesitantly."

The shrill of the phone woke her, and startled, she jumped up to answer it.

"Just making sure you're up," came Blake's cheery voice over the line.

"Do you still want to go? Did you hear that storm earlier this morning?" *He could sleep through anything*, she remembered.

"Storm? No. Are you sure that you weren't dreaming? It's just a little overcast is all. Come on, Brenda, if you don't want to go, just say so."

"I *want* to, it's just I thought—oh never mind. If we're going, I'd better get off this phone and get dressed," she told him.

"You're not dressed? What are you wearing?"

"Never mind. *Goodbye* Blake." She could hear his laughter as she ended the call. Seeing him these past few days and finding out that he wasn't involved with anyone else gave her hope. The time they'd spent together was like a wonderful dream—one she hoped never to waken from.

When Blake arrived, he seemed in better spirits than he had all week. "How come you're so perky this morning?"

she asked him. "You weren't that morning we went riding," she pointed out, miffed.

"This is different."

"Why?" She thought she knew, but wanted to hear his answer.

"Because we're going flying, that's why," he answered impatiently as though that should explain everything. And to someone who knew him as well as she did, it made sense.

"I see. Now that we're doing something *you* want to do, you're happy.

"Yup." He grinned.

Brenda sat on the passenger side of the sleek navy blue and white Cessna 150 and watched Blake walk around outside doing the pre-flight check. Finally, he released the tie-downs and climbed into the pilot's seat next to her.

"This plane reminds me of your old Triumph Alpine sports car," she told him. "It only has room for two in it."

"Yeah, cozy, isn't it?" He grinned then reached over and patted her knee which almost touched his. There wasn't enough room to shift away from him—even if she'd wanted to.

Brenda watched, fascinated, when Blake pushed some buttons on the instrument panel and the engine coughed, whined and roared to life as the single propeller on the nose spun in a fast blur. He pushed the throttle in and taxied the small plane out to the takeoff and landing strip. She watched his feet maneuver the rudder pedals that looked like a car's gas and brake pedals. He kept the yoke still. The yoke reminded her of half of a sports car's small steering wheel. There was also a yoke and pedals on her side of the plane.

"This is just like driver's training in high school," she observed aloud, looking at the two sets of controls.

"These small Cessna 150s and 152s are popular training planes for wannabe pilots," he replied without turning his head. Brenda didn't want to interrupt his concentration, and tried to keep her feet away from the pedals, which forced her even closer to Blake. Meanwhile, he turned some knobs on the panel, seemed satisfied when a particular set of numbers showed on two of the dials, and then picked up the microphone while he listened to what she thought sounded like a bunch of static garble. But Blake spoke into the mic, rattling off the airplane's call number—which she knew was painted on its side—and requested permission from the control tower for takeoff. She thought she could hear their plane's number repeated back and some other words along with it, through the crackle in Blake's headphones. But he appeared to understand, for he replied and replaced the mic on its holder. The plane taxied between the yellow lines of a paved pathway, from its parking spot to the runway, then stopped.

"What are we waiting for?" she ventured to ask, afraid to interrupt his concentration.

"Oh yeah. You need to put your headphones on. They're over there," he said and pointed, then picked up the mic again. She heard a deep rumble and loud roar and saw a Boeing jumbo jet pass them. Blake spoke into the mic again, and then it was their turn on the runway. He pushed in the throttle and the small aircraft picked up speed. It moved forward faster and faster, until the plane's nose rose up and Brenda could no longer see over it. She looked out the window on her side and saw the ground drop out from under them at the same time she felt the plane lift. Her stomach seemed to fall, the way it did on a roller coaster ride.

Brenda watched the buildings and cars grow smaller and smaller. Soon she felt as though they were on top of the world, with blue sky above and below them. They flew past the populous areas, and then far below, she saw a river. The muddy water looked like a tiny winding ribbon of deep, rich, chocolate milk. The rest of the landscape was a mass of melding shades of greens and browns as they flew over a forest and then fields. Seen from the sky, the whole landscape looked incredible.

"This is awesome," she breathed.

Then they flew over a lake. The water was a deep, deep blue that grew darker as they moved farther away from the shore. Sailboats looked like tiny white blobs.

Brenda turned to Blake and found him watching her with amusement. "Do you like it?" he asked.

"It's wonderful. I love this," she answered. "You can see everything so much closer and in more detail than on a commercial jet flight."

"And you've never had your own private pilot, have you?" he asked, then leaned over and kissed her.

Brenda couldn't pretend indifference to his kiss. She shifted in her seat, strained against the restrictive seatbelt and kissed him back. Blake didn't say anything, but turned toward the instrument panel and flipped a switch. "What's that for?" she asked him.

"I put the plane on 'automatic pilot.' "

"Is that *safe*?" she asked.

"*I'm* not worried, but whether *you're* 'safe' or not, I can't say." He laughed and reached for her. "Take your seatbelt off."

With fumbling fingers, she attempted to obey. Blake, always the impatient one, reached across and unbuckled it for her. He drew her closer, enveloped her in his arms and held her tight against his chest. Then he kissed her. It started off gently, and then became something...more. He'd wound his arms around her back, pulling her even closer, and ground his lips against hers. Abruptly, he pulled back and just stared at her.

"I've wanted to do that all week," he muttered.

"But you seemed so remote and indifferent at times," she said, still not sure she could trust him.

"I know," he said quietly.

The plane, which had been running along smoothly, suddenly bumped up and down several times.

"Why is it doing that?" Brenda asked, worried.

"Just an air pocket. But I'd better take it off autopilot."

"Where are we going, Blake?"

"I thought we'd fly down to Ocean Shores for lunch, if that sounds good to you." When she nodded, he continued, "Would you like to fly the plane?"

"Fly?" She hesitated, and then shook her head. "No, I don't think so."

"Oh, come on. I'm right here. It's just like driver's training in high school like you said. The instructors never let you wreck the car, did they?"

"I know, but..."

"It's fun."

"Yeah, it looks like it," she agreed, her indecision wavering. "Well, okay, I'll try it, " she said, giving in. She put her hands tentatively on the yoke. "Now what?"

"You want to keep the plane flying at a constant speed, straight and level. So, if the nose starts to rise, pull the yoke toward you. See?" He demonstrated. "Now you try it."

Brenda clutched the yoke tighter, trembling a bit as she tried to emulate Blake. "Like this?"

"Just a little bit. It doesn't take much...that's it. Good. And if you want to pull the nose back down, just ease it forward a bit." He demonstrated again, and then showed her how to bank the plane to the left or right by turning the yoke.

"What if I want to fly faster?"

"If you want to increase the speed, you just push in the throttle here," he said, showing her. "It's like a gas pedal and brake all in one."

"What are the pedals for, then? I saw you using them before we took off."

"That's the rudder. It turns the plane on the ground—like a steering wheel." He turned to her and laughed. "What's the matter?"

"It's so confusing. Then there's all those gauges and controls and switches on the instrument panel. This is way worse than learning to drive a car with a stick."

He laughed and urged her to take the yoke again. "Go ahead."

Brenda gripped each side of the yoke tight and turned. The plane slanted right sharply. She looked at Blake, frantic, but he just smiled and refused to touch the wheel in front of him. When Brenda got the plane righted again, he told her to make it fly higher.

"I don't think I can."

"Yes you can. You're doing great."

"I'll try." She did it. She was still scared, but thrilled at the same time—amazed at all that she controlled with her hands. She was flying a plane! She pushed in the throttle, at Blake's direction, and felt the airplane respond with a thrust of power. If only it wasn't so complicated—the rest of it—she'd love to learn to fly. She looked at Blake, and knew her eyes must be shining.

"See? You like it, don't you?" He grinned at her.

"Yes, I admit, I really do."

"Maybe we'll turn you into a pilot yet. It only takes forty hours of flight training. But now, I'd better take over so we can get there and back in time." He took the yoke and they flew steadily until Brenda could see the ocean. The water was a dazzling green-blue and the long gray-white beaches stretched out below them for miles.

It seemed to Brenda that Blake purposely followed a pair of seagulls, as they swooped and soared in the wind. The plane sunk lower and lower until it appeared as though they would skim the water. "Blake, what are you doing?" she asked in alarm.

"Trying to get a better view," he answered.

"You're like a kid with a toy. Don't you think we're close enough to the water? Last time I looked, this wasn't a seaplane."

"We're going to land on that beach up ahead."

"What!" Have you ever done this before?" *Maybe that injury did something to his brain—his ability to make good decisions.*

"Sure. Lots of times"

"Lots of times?"

"Okay, maybe twice. Trust me."

It wasn't even a bad landing, Brenda thought as she gritted her teeth, and her fingers turned red, then white on red, where she gripped the armrest on her seat. The plane barely bounced and a flash of yellow blurred past. When the plane stopped, she looked back and saw that the yellow blur was a windsock. She usually saw them at airstrips. "Oh, I guess you really *can* land here," she said, surprised.

"I guess I *did*," Blake laughed at her, then once again, leaned over and gave her a kiss. This time it was a much gentler kiss. She kissed him back. After a time, he pulled away. "I guess we'd better go get lunch."

"Yeah, I guess we should." She sighed.

The beach was nearly deserted when they headed back to the plane after lunch. Blake took Brenda's hand, and led her to the water's edge. They took off their shoes and socks and rolled up their pant legs, then waded into the water. Brenda felt like a carefree child. It was a beautiful sunny day on the beach and she was with Blake. With no one else to see her, she delighted in jumping the waves. Accidentally—of course—she splashed water on Blake, which caused him to seek revenge and a splashing war followed, until, "Blake, stop! I'm getting all wet!" she shrieked.

He made a couple more half-hearted splashes at her then held up his hands in surrender.

They walked away from the water carrying their shoes, past the plane, and up the beach in the other direction. Their path was sometimes blocked by rocks and boulders, and Blake took hold of her hand, but she found it was easier to scramble over them on her own, so after awhile, she let go of his hand.

He climbed over another boulder, took her hand again and this time didn't let go. "Let's find a place to sit." He led her a little ways farther, and then pulled her down to sit with him on the sand, their backs resting against a large rock.

They sat in silence, the background sound of the ocean waves lapping against the sand dulled behind their rock shelter. Seagulls circled lazily overhead. Her spirits buoyed by the good feelings from such a marvelous day—sunny skies, the flight, Blake's teaching her to fly the plane, lunch at the restaurant on the water, wading and playing in the ocean, strolling on the beach, and holding hands—gave Brenda the nerve to say, "Your sister thinks I left *you*. So does your mother. Did you tell them that?"

"No...well, not really," he answered.

Brenda frowned. "Then, how did she get that idea?" she asked, and looked at him. It seemed to her that he actually blushed.

Blake didn't say anything for a moment as though considering his answer. "The truth is, Amber just assumed it and I...I didn't enlighten her. She must have told Mom." He looked away.

"Why not?" Brenda asked, shocked. No wonder his sister acted so cool toward her.

"I don't know." Blake leaned over and started to draw circles in the sand. "I guess I just felt so mad at you for the way you treated my mom.

"If you felt that way, why did you come to see me after the wedding? Why would you want to see me again after all this time?"

Blake stayed quiet for a moment. "I wasn't going to. I wasn't even going to stop and see you that day at the airport. Alan was supposed to meet me there before he flew home, but when he didn't show, I thought I'd check to see if you were working, and stop by to say hello. And then, I don't know...honestly Brenda, I don't know what it is, but there's something holding us together."

"But you've been so hot and cold with me this week."

"I know. I've been at war with myself, fighting my feelings for you," he admitted. "I alternate between trying to get closer to you and trying to hold you at arm's length."

"What are you afraid of?" she asked softly.

Blake looked out toward the ocean. "Maybe that nothing's changed. That we'll get back together and it won't work—again, I guess. My heart was broken when I walked away, Brenda. It took a long time to heal."

"Why *did* you break up with me, Blake? I've never really understood."

He laughed humorlessly. "Well, I think *that's* obvious. I finally realized that you didn't want to be around my family, that you don't like them."

"*What?*" she gasped. "Whatever gave you that idea?"

He stared at her. "You never wanted to go to my parents' house for the holidays. You always made up some reason not to. And when Amber told me…" He stopped suddenly.

"Go on. Amber told you…what?"

"Well, she told me about all the times she and Mom invited you over to the house and you turned them down," he said, rather reluctantly, she thought.

"Blake, you grew up in a large, close-knit family—your dad, mom, brother and sister, two sets of grandparents, aunts, uncles, and cousins. My family—after my mom left us and divorced my dad—was just me, my brother Tim, and my dad. Both my parents were only-children and their parents passed away before I was old enough to remember them.

"Your holiday gatherings were filled with laughter, food and lots of people—I counted twenty-five of your family, friends and neighbors that last time. And everyone sat down to dinner at the table and your mom said grace before we ate. My holiday dinners were just the three of us. I did most of the cooking when I was old enough to read a cookbook. Dad and Tim came into the kitchen, loaded their plates and plopped back down in front of the TV again to watch their games. I took my plate, sat on my bed and watched *It's a Wonderful Life*, on my TV while I ate.

"So the first time I went to a holiday dinner at your house, I felt...overwhelmed."

"Well, yeah, I figured that. You'd told me holidays were quiet at your house growing up," Blake acknowledged. "But I thought you'd adjust. I guess I was wrong..." his voice trailed off, and a pained look crossed his face.

"I'd told Mom how things were for you, that your mom left, and it was just you and Tim and your dad. She felt bad and wanted to make things special for you...make you feel part of the family. Maybe she was a little overbearing, but I know she didn't mean to be. She has a good heart. If you'd just given her a chance..." his voice trailed off again. "Anyway, I tried to be understanding, but my family's important to me—"

"I know, Blake. I realize that," Brenda said quietly.

"—and the thought that to be with you meant that I'd never be part of my large, extended family for the rest of my life, didn't sit well. I held on, hoping that things would change, but they didn't. And, well, you know the rest."

"And yet, you moved away," she said.

"Yeah. I did. The, ironic thing is, the thought of those big family gatherings without you caused me to move away from everyone I loved."

Brenda sighed. "Oh Blake, I should have told you this a long time ago. I didn't dislike your family; I *loved* being part of your family." Blake looked at her in disbelief, but she couldn't blame him. She rushed to explain. "It was your mom—"

"I know that Brenda," he sounded wary.

"No, you don't understand...I was afraid," she whispered.

"Afraid of my *mom*?" he asked her in amazement. "She's the nicest, kindest—"

"I *know*, Blake. What I mean is, I was afraid to get close to her, afraid to lose her," she admitted in a quiet voice, tears hiding under her eyelids. "I was afraid to lose the only real mom I've ever known."

Blake stared at her as if stunned. Finally he spoke."I've been wrong about you, Brenda. I'm so sorry. Then he leaned over, reached out and folded her into his arms. She'd never had a better hug.

High-pitched children's voices reached them. Blake dropped his arms, leaned back and stood up. He held out a hand to her. "I wish we could stay longer, but we need to get the plane back by two o'clock. I only have it rented till then."

She hated to leave the quiet beach behind and regretted that their time together was almost over. "Do you think you might take me flying again?"

"Sure, but maybe you'll be a pilot yourself someday." He grinned at her.

They hurried back down the beach to the plane, and Brenda allowed Blake to pull her after him. But when she slipped on a sand-covered boulder and lost her balance, it caused her to yank back on his hand. In the midst of clambering over the next boulder himself, Blake was caught off guard. His foot slid down between some rocks and stayed there, and they both tumbled down to the sand.

Brenda got up first, spitting the sand out of her mouth, and dusting it off her sweatshirt and jeans. Blake got up a little more slowly and when he took a few steps, Brenda saw him limp slightly. "Are you okay?"

"Yeah, just a little stiff, I think."

"Are you sure you're okay?"

"I'm fine." He looked at his watch. "We'd better go." He reached for her hand again, and Brenda followed. His gait seemed awkward to her, but she didn't have much time to observe him long before they reached the plane.

Once they were ready to fly, Blake taxied the plane back down the beach and opened the throttle. This time Brenda watched the air-speed indicator with interest. She saw that when it reached fifty-five knots, he pulled back on the yoke, the nose lifted and the Cessna lifted off the ground.

"Brenda?"

She'd been so absorbed in her thoughts and the view, she started when she suddenly heard Blake's voice.

"Yeah?"

"I don't want to frighten you, but..."

His words alone were enough to frighten her. She turned and gave him her full attention.

"What?"

"I'm afraid you were right. It *is* too soon; I shouldn't have taken us out flying."

She noticed that his face looked pale.

"What's the matter?"

"I must have torn open the stitches when I fell on those rocks. My leg's bleeding again and I feel kinda dizzy. I'm not sure I can land the plane."

"You're not kidding, are you?"

"No. I think...you'll need to do it, Brenda."

"I can't!" She looked at him in horror. She felt even further shaken by the sight of his white face.

"Yes, you can. You have to..." his voice trailed off and seemed to fight against pain. Afraid to, she looked down at the bandage on his leg. It was bright red.

"Oh Blake," she whispered, and as usual, felt light-headed at the sight of blood.

He nodded. "It won't be that bad. Most of your work will be with your feet. I'll talk you through it. Remember when I used to let you shift my car while I drove? It'll kinda' be like that." He grabbed her hand. "We'll land this thing together, okay?"

Brenda trembled with fear, but she nodded.

Blake called the tower and told them what was happening and Brenda heard a voice say they would clear the field for an emergency landing.

Her heart raced. Her hands shook and slid on the wheel with nervousness, and her legs trembled, but she forced them to obey. Then she blocked out everything and listened only to Blake's instructions.

All too soon, they approached Boeing Field and time to land. The wheels hit the ground with a decided thump and the plane bounced a couple times, and then they were speeding down a foam-covered runway.

"Apply the brakes!" Blake called out to her sharply, and cut the power. Brenda moved her toes up so they covered the tops of the pedals and pushed down with all her strength.

And then, finally, it was over. She looked shakily at Blake. He grasped her hands with his right one and held it.

A crowd gathered on the runway and several people broke away and approached their small plane. An ambulance pulled up, its red lights flashing and someone opened the plane's door.

"You did it, Carrot," Blake smiled weakly at her.

"*We* did it Blake," she corrected him. "Together."

"I love you, Brenda Burke. Do you suppose you could ever forgive me for the way I've treated you?"

"I believe I could. love you too."

And with a crowd of people staring at them, and EMTs waiting to take Blake to the hospital, she leaned over, put her arms around his neck, and kissed him.

Epilogue

Earlier that morning, Brenda walked into the Preston's steamy kitchen and found it filled with laughter and mostly—except for Blake's dad making his special dressing—female voices. A belonging she'd never before experienced flooded through her. *This, is how a Christmas dinner should be—family, and even friends, getting together to create a meal with love and laughter.*

Brenda saw Amber look up from the cutting board where she chopped vegetables and smiled at her. She gestured to the apple pie—Blake's favorite—Brenda prepared at home the night before, using Mrs. Preston's recipe. "Mmm, smells good."

Now, as she stirred her mulled cider with a cinnamon stick, and chatted with Blake's Aunt Kathy and his cousin, Amy, Brenda paused to listen to the strains of "O Holy Night," that drifted in from the piano in the living room. She smiled when Blake left the piano and walked into the kitchen. He gave his mom a hug around her waist with one arm, and then reached around her with the other and grabbed a piece of ham off the platter. Mrs. Preston slapped his hand as though he was a naughty teenager.

"Aww Ma..." Blake protested. "I'm hungry."

"You'll just have to wait like everyone else. You're as bad as your nephew," his mother chided him, while Brenda and the women in the kitchen laughed.

"Okay, I'll bother someone else." He pouted, moved away from his mother and stopped next to Brenda. "Hi, babe. What'cha doing?" He read the words on his mother's frilly red and green Christmas apron that Brenda borrowed to keep her good clothes clean. "'Kiss Me Now and Avoid the Holiday Rush'? With pleasure." He leaned over and gave her a kiss.

"I'm so happy that *all* of my children are home with me for the holidays," Blake's mother said and beamed.

"So are we, Mom, "Blake agreed and looked at Brenda, who smiled.

She finally had a heart for the holidays.

MARILYN CONNER MILES

PERFECT PAIR

Chapter One

Amber closed the cardboard box, and looked around the empty cubicle one last time. She'd plucked all of her personal possessions off the mauve-colored fabric walls and cleared off her desk. She picked up her purse, draped it over her shoulder and lifted the box off the desk with both hands, balancing the small potted plant on top. She glanced around the large room filled with identical cubicles and then, eyes downcast, walked down the long corridor and out to the reception area.

"Well, I guess that's it," she told Stacy, before she realized the receptionist was speaking into the mouthpiece of her headphones. Stacy held up a finger.

Amber hoped the receptionist would hurry. She felt so embarrassed to have lost her job, she'd gone in early, hoping to pack up her things and get out of the building before anyone saw her. But she'd already turned in her keys and needed to wait for someone to unlock the law firm's door. She felt relieved that Stacy was the first one to arrive.

The receptionist turned to her and frowned. "I'm so sorry, Amber. I'll miss you. You'll stay in touch won't you, and let us know how you're doing and where you're working? Maybe we could meet for lunch someday soon."

Amber managed a brief smile. "Sure Stacy. I'd like that," she said but doubted she would.

"Well, you know my number," Stacy said with a wistful half-smile.

"Yeah, I have it memorized," Amber replied and was about to say more, but just then the phone rang, so she waved at Stacy and headed to the front door.

A blast of wintry wind greeted her as she struggled to pull the heavy door open with her arms full of the box, plant and the purse which slid off her shoulder. A hand reached out and grabbed the door and held it open for her. She looked up. Oh great. It was Barbara, the office manager—the one who told her they were letting her go.

"Goodbye, Amber. Good luck with your job search. Be sure to get signed up for unemployment right away. We'll get your final check out to you soon." The woman actually smiled as she said it.

"Thanks," Amber mumbled as she walked through the door and out to the street where she'd parked her car at a meter.

Amber struggled to get the box and plant up the two flights of stairs and then open the door of her apartment. She wanted to sit down and cry, but knew she needed to sign up for unemployment benefits as Barbara reminded her. At least she didn't have to leave the apartment to do it. She plopped down on the sofa and hunched over her laptop. She brought up the website and filled in the information…and then reality hit. She would not be able to afford her rent on the amount shown on the screen. She had no real savings to speak of. She'd lost her job and her home. Now what?

She picked up the phone and called her mother's work number.

"Hi, Mom."

"Amber?" Why are you home? Are you sick today?"

"I suppose you could say that," Amber replied. She took a deep breath. "Mom, I got laid off." She waited for her mother to say something, but it was quiet on the other end for what seemed like forever, until her mother finally spoke.

"Oh honey, I'm so sorry. Do you want to come over for dinner tonight and talk about it?"

"Okay Mom, thanks."

Food seemed to be her mother's way of dealing with any situation—good or bad. Amber didn't really want to face her family, or anyone else, with her self-esteem at an all time low, but she supposed it was a good time to ask her parents if she could move in with them for awhile. "I'll let you go for now. See you then." Amber sighed as she pushed the Off button. Better start looking for work.

The rest of the morning Amber sent out emails to everyone she could think of who might know of a paralegal job available. She also applied online for several jobs on various job websites. When she tired of staring unblinkingly at the screen, she logged off her computer, headed for the kitchen and opened the refrigerator. "Hmm. Not much here. I need to go grocery shopping." She reached for a small carton of yogurt, shut the door and grabbed a spoon. As she scraped the spoon around the small carton for the last bite, her phone rang.

She didn't recognize the number on her cell phone screen and hoped it might be a call back from someone who'd received her resume. Maybe they wanted to set up a phone or in-person interview. If she got a job she wouldn't have to give up her apartment and this whole nightmare would be over.

"Hello, this is Amber," she said into the phone, trying not to sound desperate.

"Hi, kiddo."

"Blake? What's this phone number? Where are you?" she asked her brother who lived and worked in San Francisco.

"This is my new phone number. I'm with Brenda right now."

"How is my future sister-in-law? She flew down to see you?"

"No, I'm in Seattle. I'm back for good, right hon?" Amber heard a female voice respond in the background.

"I bet Brenda's over-the-moon."

"Yeah." Amber could hear the smile in his voice. "Hey, sis, we're going to be at Mom and Dad's for dinner tonight. Will you be there?"

"When did you talk to Mom last?"

"Last night."

"Ohh...well, you haven't heard my news,

then." She looked at her watch. "Oops, I gotta get ready. See you at dinner."

"What news? Wait. Don't hang up." Amber could hear her brother's voice but she said a quick goodbye, ended the call, and sank down into a chair.

When Amber reached her parents' house in Bellevue, across the lake from Seattle, she saw Brenda's car in the driveway and another car on the curb that she was pretty sure belonged to her oldest brother, Carson. Yup, there was a car seat in the back. So, the whole family would be there tonight. She sighed. Mom rallied the troops.

As Amber looked around the table, she smiled to see Blake and Brenda together. It hadn't always been that way. They'd broken up six years ago because of a total misunderstanding. Blake broke up with her, but led his family to believe Brenda broke up with him. He'd taken a job in San Francisco shortly after and moved there. Amber supposed he'd thought he'd never see Brenda again, but he hadn't thought about the effect it had on his family back home in Washington State.

When he came home for a friend's wedding, Brenda was there—as were Amber and her parents. And then an accident forced them all together. The person who probably should have been the most unforgiving, Amber's mother, was actually the first to forgive Brenda. Once Amber learned the truth, she found that she actually liked Brenda. Amber didn't think she could ever forgive a man the way Brenda forgave her brother for his lie—or fib, or something of omission, or whatever he called it. But then, Amber reminded herself, she'd never been in love.

Everyone drifted into the family room with its big screen TV and the grandkids' toy box. But when their youngest child got cranky, her sister-in-law turned to Carson and said, "It's your turn." Her brother rose from the family room sofa to change his son's diaper and Amber saw her chance.

"Mom, can I talk to you for a minute?" She'd hoped to get her mother aside earlier, but this was her first chance, as everyone wanted to talk about Blake's and Brenda's plans now that he'd moved back.

"Sure. Why don't you help me in the kitchen?" her mother replied.

Once they'd stepped into the kitchen and the swinging wooden louvered doors closed behind them, Amber told herself, *No time like the present. Just get straight to the point.*

"Mom, without my job, I won't be able to pay my rent or make ends meet, so I was wondering if I could stay with you and Dad for awhile until I get back on my feet," she said in rush, then looked hopefully at her mother. But she didn't like the frown that formed on her mother's lips. Uh-oh.

"Honey, you know we'd be happy to have you, but…"

It was Amber's turn to frown. *But?*

"...Carson and Kim and the boys will be staying with us for...actually, I don't know how long."

"What? Why?" She hadn't seen this coming. She'd just assumed...

"When they started the remodel on the master bath, the construction workers found a huge leak under the tub and then a major mold problem. It's so bad that they have to bring in some "mold remediation" experts and get out of the house while it's being worked on. They were going to go to a hotel, but of course your dad and I persuaded them to come here. They'll have the guestroom and den. I supposed you could sleep on a sofa in the family room, but we'd planned to use that as the boys' playroom. Oh dear."

"That's okay, Mom. Don't worry. I'm sure I can couch surf with a friend for awhile." She tried to sound upbeat, but inside, she wondered if what she told her mother was true. One of her friends lived with a boyfriend Amber didn't like, and the other lived in a small studio where the couch was a futon and that's what her friend slept on. Now she didn't know what to do. "Well, is there any room in the garage for me to store some stuff?"

"Oh sure." Her mother looked relieved. "Ask your dad."

Amber quietly set the table in the dining room and started to bring platters of food from the kitchen, when Brenda joined her, grabbing a dish from one of her hands. They worked in silence for awhile after that until her mother asked her to call everyone in to dinner.

Amber waited until dessert to tell the rest of the family that she'd lost her job. She got sympathetic murmurs, and "sorry to hear that, Amber," from the adults.

"If you lost your job, Aunt Amber, I can help you find it again," her five-year-old nephew, Max, piped up. "Mom says I'm really good at finding things I lost."

"Well, thank you, Max, but I'm not even sure I want to find that job. I think I need to get a new one. In fact, I just might try to find something entirely different."

"But what will you do, Amber?" her sister-in-law Kim asked with a puzzled look on her face. I thought you went to school to be a paralegal."

Amber sighed. "Yeah, I did, but...I'm not sure that's what I want to do anymore. It's pretty stressful. As for what I will do...I really don't know."

There was a general silence around the table, until the baby began to fuss. Kim rose from her chair and unbuckled him from the high chair and carried him away from the table. Then Amber's mother rose and cleared the dessert plates from the table, and Blake joined her. Brenda started to get up, but Blake told her to stay; she and Amber had already done their part and it was the men's turn to help out in the kitchen.

"Thanks, bro," Carson said with a frown. But he gestured to Max. "Come on son, you're not too young to learn how things work at Grandma's house."

When it was just the two of them still seated at the table, Brenda turned to Amber and patted her arm. "Don't let it get you down. I've been through layoffs. It's no fun, and rather scary, but sometimes it can lead to something better."

Amber couldn't imagine that.

Chapter Two

Two weeks later, when Amber woke, she didn't get out of bed. She stared up at the ceiling, lost in thought, until she heard her cell phone buzz on the nightstand.

Call me, Brenda texted.

Amber turned on her bedside lamp and punched in Brenda's number.

"Have you found anything yet?"

"No." Amber sighed. "It's pretty discouraging. I send resumes and no one even responds. I've had a couple short phone interviews, but then I don't get called in for an in-person interview."

"I think I have an idea of a job for you. One of my coworkers told me about it."

"I appreciate it, Brenda, I do, but I'm not interested in working for an airline."

"It's not with the airline. And it's just a temporary job, something you can do while you decide what you want to do next. You'd get paid and have a place to live and…well, I'd better not say anything more until I talk to my coworker."

Amber felt intrigued…and mystified. "Okay, thanks."

"I'll talk to him as soon as I can and call you tonight? Brenda asked.

"Sure. I'll be home."

Amber tried to drum up enthusiasm for the job search, and half-heartedly surfed the Net, then later that morning, walked out to the mailbox to see if her final check had come. When she sorted through the mail, she didn't see any check, only bills. She walked back to her apartment and called the law firm, glad that Stacy answered the phone.

"Oh hi, Amber," the other woman said. "How are you? Did you get a job?"

"No, unfortunately, I need to talk to Payroll. I haven't received my check yet."

"Gosh, that's terrible. Here, I'll put you through." The line clicked before she could say another word. But then it rang four times and when it finally picked up, Amber took a breath to speak, but realized she'd gotten voicemail. She left her name and number and a brief message, then hung up.

Might as well be productive while she waited. Amber booted up her computer again and searched some more, then as time passed with no call back, she played a couple games of Solitaire. Her stomach growled so she walked over to the refrigerator and grabbed a yogurt. Just as she raised the spoon to her lips, the phone buzzed.

"Amber, can you meet me this afternoon around three-thirty? I'll pick you up at your apartment," Brenda said, sounding out of breath."

"Yes, but why?"

"I have to talk fast, but here's the deal: one of the pilots and his wife are on vacation in Europe, so they had a neighbor taking care of their animals. She just broke her leg and can't get around much, and they need to find another house-and-pet sitter. I told him about your current situation and he suggested I take you up there and show you the place."

"Up there?"

"North of Seattle."

"Well, I don't know…but I guess it wouldn't hurt to take a look," Amber replied hesitantly. "Sure, come and get me. Thanks Brenda."

For the rest of the day she looked through her bills, wrote out a few checks, balanced her checkbook, and got further depressed. By three o'clock, she felt ready to get out of her apartment. She could use a change of scenery. She didn't know what she should wear, but assumed she'd meet the neighbor, and that it was kind of a job interview, so she decided just to go with some nice pants and blouse—and a warm coat. It was damp from the fog and chilly outside.

When Brenda arrived, Amber closed and locked her apartment door and hurried outside to get into the warm car.

"I hope we get there before dark. I've only been there once before at a party, but that was in the summer, and I'm not sure I remember exactly how to get there." Brenda frowned.

"Did you put the address in the GPS on your smart phone?"

"No, I didn't have time. It was really busy at SeaTac today and the fog made things worse."

"Do you have the address? I'll put it into my

phone."

Brenda fumbled around in her purse with the hand not on the steering wheel. "Here."

Amber grabbed the small scrap of paper and typed the address into her phone until she came to the city. "Stanwood?"

"Yeah, you know, by Camano Island. Lots of people had summer cabins there when I was a kid, but it's more developed now."

"Yes, but that's way north of Seattle. The GPS shows fifty miles from my apartment."

"Sure, but you'd be staying there. It's not like you'd have to commute."

"What if I have to go to Seattle for an interview?"

"It's not the end of the Earth. You can drive in for an interview and maybe do some errands or something while you're in town."

"I guess. Besides, I'm just looking at this opportunity, right?"

"Yes, but I think you'll like the peace, the serenity of staying in the country."

To Amber, it seemed as though they just kept driving and driving north on Interstate 5, past shopping malls and empty stretches of land, then a casino and then more vacant land.

"There's the exit, Brenda." When they left the freeway, they were really out in the country, as they passed field after field of farmland. "Where are we going?"

"We're almost there." Soon they passed through a tiny one-street town with a café and a couple stores and then made a turn up a steep hill past two more dairy farms. Brenda slowed the car down and peered at the street signs. "What does the GPS show?"

"It says we've reached our destination, but these things aren't always reliable." Amber frowned.

"No, I think this is it. I remember the red barn mailbox." Brenda pulled the car off the narrow country road onto some gravel in front of a gate with a padlock. "Let me call the number Bob gave me for the neighbor." She picked up her cell phone and punched in some numbers, while Amber gazed around.

There was a long, circular gravel driveway that passed by a garage or barn—she couldn't tell which—and a large carport that housed an RV. The house sat way back off the street and appeared to be made out of logs. But it wasn't a little log cabin; it was more like a lodge.

"She's coming right over," Brenda said, looking down the road toward the neighbor's house. Shortly after that, another car pulled into the driveway, and a teenage girl emerged slowly from the passenger side.

"Hi, I'm Mandy," she said, then turned around and pulled some crutches through the rolled down window and off the car's back seat. "I'll call you when I'm ready, Mom," she said to the driver and held up her cell phone with one hand, while she leaned on the crutches with the other.

She held up a crutch, then hopped over to the gate and unlocked the padlock with a small key, then hopped again and swung the gate wide open. "Park anywhere." She waved her hand around the gravel driveway.

"We can wait for you to close the gate and give you a ride up to the house," Brenda offered."

"No, that's okay," the girl replied. "I'm pretty good with these." She nodded at the crutches.

Amber saw that Mandy was right about her abilities with the crutches. By the time Brenda parked the car, and they got out, Mandy stood next to them.

"Mandy, I'm Brenda—Bob's coworker—and this is my soon-to-be sister-in-law, Amber. She's the one interested in the job."

"What happened to you?" Amber asked.

"Oh, just a little accident. It's not too bad, but I can't get around well enough to take care of the animals with these. I sure hope you can start right away." Mandy smiled. "Let's start with the outdoor animals."

"Outdoor animals?" Amber asked.

"The horses, the cows, the goats, the chickens…well, you'll see. Follow me," she said and swung herself on the crutches toward the barn/garage.

Amber looked at Brenda. "How many animals are there, anyway?" she asked her future sister-in-law in an accusatory tone. "I'd pictured a dog or two and a cat…maybe a bird, or gold fish." Amber narrowed her eyes.

"Well, I really don't know. I suppose they could have acquired more since I was here for that party last summer. Come on, we'd better go. Mandy's waiting for us." Brenda hurried off.

"Okay, but I'm just looking, you know," Amber grumbled as she followed.

Mandy opened the sliding doors on the big building, and inside Amber saw several stalls. Two horses flung their heads over their half-doors with stalks of hay sticking out of their mouths. "This one's Sugar and this is Spice. They're Quarter Horses," Mandy told them. "And over here, are Heidi and Gretchen, Brown Swiss cows." She gestured as she moved along the row of stalls. "And this is Buddy and here's Belle. They're Nigerian dwarf goats. Outside, in the pen is Jake. He's a Rhode Island Red rooster, and Jackie the hen is an Australorp." She pointed through the open door of the stall to a little house in an enclosure. "And the turkeys, Tommy and Taffy, are wandering around here somewhere..."

"So, are these all the 'pets'?" Amber asked.

"The outside ones...well, the dogs are usually outside too, but I put them inside before you got here. Otherwise, they might not have let you in the gate," Mandy told them cheerfully. "I fed everyone before you got here, with my mom's help. Oh, and there's Woolie. She gestured to the pasture. He's the only sheep they have. Come on, let's go to the house and you can meet the others." She patted one of the horses on its neck, then swung off on the crutches and headed toward the barn door.

"What is this, an ark?" Amber whispered to Brenda. "Is your friend named Noah?"

Brenda shook her head and laughed. "Everything does seem to come in pairs—even the humans; there's just Bob and his wife, Nancy—well, except for Woolie. No, it's just a mini-farm."

They followed Mandy out of the barn and to the house. Amber could see, now that she was closer, that the house was not made of logs, but it still had that rustic lodge look. As they walked up the wide wooden steps to the deck, she noted the tall windows in the front, and the way the middle section of the house rose to a high peak. It looked as though the deck might wrap around the house. She could see it on at least three sides.

Brenda must have noticed her staring at the house, and said, "Beautiful, isn't it? I remember Nancy telling me that it's called 'Post and Beam' construction and that it's all made out of Western Red Cedar. Wait till you see the inside."

Something let out a strange sound. Amber spun around. "What is that? It looks like a vulture." She pointed.

"It think it's a female turkey," Brenda replied. "That must be Taffy."

Just then, Amber heard a loud *woof* followed by a higher-pitched *woof-woof-woof.* Mandy pushed another key into the door's lock and said, "Let me go in first, and then I'll introduce you to the dogs." She stuck her crutch in first, then crooned in a sing-song voice, "Bruiser, Samantha, it's me, Mandy." Then she walked inside.

Bruiser? What the heck am I getting into?

When a long-haired black and white dog

stepped out, Amber gasped. It looked like a wolf.

"Samantha is a Siberian Husky," Brenda told Amber. The dog must have recognized a friendly voice, and gave Brenda's hand a big slurp with her large pink tongue. Then she sat down and gave them a canine grin.

Mandy stuck her head out the open door. "I see you met Samantha. Isn't she a lover? Come on in and meet Bruiser and the cats."

Amber looked at Brenda. "After you." But for a moment, when she stepped inside the door, she forgot all about the brutish dog she expected to see. She felt in awe of the home's open design interior—high, vaulted wood ceilings with huge, exposed beams, beautiful wood-paneled walls, skylights and lots and lots of natural light even on this dark afternoon with night closing in. Stairs with a wrought iron railing led down to the sunken living room where a fireplace with a black metal stove insert glowed with a dancing fire and warmed up the huge room. A ceiling fan circled slowly overhead, distributing the heat.

To the right, on the far side of the room, a winding wrought iron staircase led up to a half-loft. Amber gazed to the left and saw an open kitchen with a large island where pots and pans dangled overhead from a metal rack suspended by long chains from the ceiling. Three captain's swivel seat bar stools with brass footrests were pulled up to the high counter on the other side of the island. The whole inside of the house had a rustic theme as well, with colorful Native American-style throw rugs scattered about on the hardwood floors, and red cowboy-style throw pillows on the leather sofas. Old West-themed prints of Indians and cowboys hung on the walls. There was even a black western saddle with silver trim perched on top of a bright Native American blanket on a wooden stand in the corner.

The sound of Mandy's voice brought her back to her purpose for being there. "Amber, this is Bruiser," she said, with one hand wrapped around the dog's collar." The large German Shepherd stared up at her. "Let him sniff you before you put out your hand, okay?" While Amber held her hand out tentatively to the dog, Mandy said, "Good boy. This is Amber."

Bruiser sniffed her hand and must have thought she was okay, because he turned his attention to Brenda and did the same with her. Meanwhile, Amber spied an orange tabby cat curled up on a dining room chair, then felt something brush against her legs. "Hi, kitty." She wanted to reach down and pet the sleek black feline, but the cat stood too close to Bruiser and she was afraid he'd get the wrong idea.

Mandy must have noticed the cat too. "Oh, and that's Shadow. Her sister, Zee—short for Zebra—is the one on the chair over there. Well, that's about it for the animals. Want to see the rest of the house?"

"Actually, Mandy, I wonder if we can sit down somewhere and talk about what the job entails," Brenda said and looked at Amber. She nodded.

"Sure," Mandy agreed. "Let's sit at the dining room table." Once they were seated at the large oval oak table on spindle back chairs, Mandy pointed to a little nook with a desk next to the kitchen. The feeding schedule is there on the desk—you know, who gets what and when—and naturally I'd go through it with you the first time." She smiled across the table at Amber. "And then there's a list of all the emergency numbers and stuff on that bulletin board." She waved her hand. "And...let's see...oh yeah, there's a calendar on the wall with appointments, like when the shoer comes—"

"Shoer?" Amber asked.

"Yeah, you know, farrier, horseshoer—although this time of the year they just get their feet trimmed." Mandy looked at Brenda, who nodded. Then the teenager gave Amber a curious look. "Have you been around horses much?"

"Well no, not really," Amber admitted and looked at Brenda, who quickly spoke up.

"I keep my horse, Carrot, in Cle Elum, so she hasn't had the chance to go riding with me." Amber thought Mandy looked somewhat reassured at that, as though at least one of them was a horseperson. However, Brenda wasn't the one interviewing for the job.

"Well thanks for all your help, Mandy. We'd better head out before it gets any later. Can we give you a ride to the gate?" Brenda offered as she rose from the chair.

"No, thanks, my mom will drive up to the house. I need to do a few things here and then lock up and set the alarm."

"Okay. I'll talk to Bob and let him know what Amber decides. Thanks again for your help." Brenda smiled at the teenager and headed for the door.

Amber stood up too, turned to Mandy and said, "Nice meeting you." As she headed to the door, both dogs were right behind her and she thought they might squeeze past her out the door, but Mandy told them to stay. Amber quickly shut the door, walked across the deck and then hurried down the steps and across the gravel drive to the car. "I'll get the gate," she told Brenda, looking around. She was surprised how dark it was, with no street lights. At least a big light on a pole in the yard came on while they were in the house.

"So what do you think about the job? Isn't it beautiful out here? And so peaceful," Brenda enthused. "This would be a great place to really think about what you want to do next."

"Yeah, I suppose…but it's still so far away from everything. And you know I don't know anything about horses…or cows or goats or chickens, for that matter. And that dog—Bruiser. Did you see the way he looked at me?"

"He's just protective. That's the way German Shepherds are. I'm sure he'd be protective of you once he got to know you and you fed him every day."

"Maybe. But what if I screwed up with the animals?"

"Mandy's next door and I'd help you

whenever I could. You'd just need to call or text me."

"Well, I'll think about it, okay?" Brenda nodded at her, and though she offered to stop somewhere to eat, Amber knew she'd want to get back and be with Blake, so she declined. Even at that time of night, the freeway was extremely busy and by the time they reached Everett, it stopped entirely. "Boy, I wouldn't want to make this commute every day," Amber observed.

"Yeah, it would be rough," Brenda agreed. "Thank goodness you wouldn't have to."

They didn't talk much the rest of the trip, but listened to the radio. Amber couldn't help but notice all the traffic reports. She'd never had a long commute to and from work and rode the bus downtown. Why would anyone move so far out that they had to go through this every day? she wondered.

Brenda dropped Amber off in front of her apartment and sped off. Just as she walked in the door, Amber heard her cell phone chirp in her purse. This time she recognized the number.

"She's on her way. She just dropped me off. The traffic was terrible up north," she said before her brother could speak.

"Okay, thanks. Are you going to take the job?" Blake asked.

"I don't know. They have a lot of animals. And it's pretty remote up there."

"Sounds great to me. Hopefully, we can buy a place in the country soon. Brenda would love to look out the window and see Carrot in the pasture."

"Yes she would. She would be great at this job too."

"Yeah, she'd love it, but she can't. I'm sure she'd be happy to give you advice, though. Well, gotta go, kiddo. I really think you should take the job, but one way or the other, you need to get back to Brenda with your decision soon."

"I know." That pressure didn't help. After they'd said goodbye, Amber realized she felt quite tired and her head ached, either from the fresh air, or the pressure to make a decision. She looked through her nearly empty refrigerator and cupboards and decided on popcorn for dinner.

The next morning, when the phone rang, Amber felt as though she'd barely slept. She'd tossed and turned and tried not to think, but it didn't work; she just kept thinking about the house-and-pet-sitting job. She'd expected a call back from the law firm's payroll department, but didn't get one.

"Sorry to call you so early, but I need to give Bob an answer, "Brenda said. "Have you decided?"

"I-I'll do it, I guess," Amber told her. "Yeah, I'll take the job. All I have to do is feed animals twice a day and then I can sit at my computer there and send out resumes, same as here."

"Great. I'll call Bob and let him know. He'll be so happy you've agreed to take the position and they don't need to worry about it anymore. How soon do you think you can be there?"

"Well, I need to pack up some stuff…"

"Don't worry about that. Just take what you need for now. You can do all that later. They really need you to start right away—oops, I have to get back to work. I'll call and make the arrangements for you to get the keys from Mandy. This is great, Amber!" Brenda exclaimed. "I think you'll love it up there," she said with enthusiasm and hung up.

Great. She'd have a place to live for a while, earn a little money, catch up on some sleep… She just wished she felt as happy about it as Brenda seemed to.

What have I done?

Chapter Three

Amber thought she could probably find the place again, but decided to use GPS anyway, and it was a good thing, because she'd forgotten some of the turns. She drove right by the gate before she recognized it by the red barn mailbox. She turned around a ways down the road in someone's driveway, drove back, pulled up in front of the gate and punched in Mandy's number on her cell phone.

"Hi, Amber? Are you at the gate?" Mandy asked.

"Yup. Do you need a ride over here?"

"Yes, please. My mom isn't home yet. We're the next house down the road."

When the girl got herself and her crutches into the car, Amber turned to her and asked, "What *really* happened to you? Skiing accident?" Silence. *Uh-oh, it must be a sore subject.*

"My mom thought I shouldn't tell you this right away, but since you asked...Bruiser and Samantha were playing—running around—and ran right into me and knocked me over. I think you should know...don't ever turn your back on them. The same thing happened to Nancy once too. She just got a sprained ankle, but I fractured a bone and sprained an ankle." She must have seen the horrified look on Amber's face because Mandy stopped talking for a minute, and then hurried to say, "You just have to be aware of where they are, is all. They didn't mean to do it. Bruiser even came over and sniffed me when I lay on the ground. He looked really sympathetic."

Amber found it hard to believe that the ferocious animal could be sympathetic, but she kept her thoughts to herself.

After Mandy handed her the keys for the gate and house and garage and other outbuildings, gave her the code for the alarm, and re-introduced her to the dogs, Amber took the teenager back home. She offered to pick her up again later when Mandy said she'd go through the first evening feeding with her, but the girl said her mom would bring her when it was time.

Amber drove back and started to get out of her car to open the gate, when she saw Bruiser running toward her. He barked at her furiously.

"Bruiser, it's me, Amber, your new best buddy." But all she got for her big smile was a growl. Then Samantha joined them, waving her big fluffy tail and smiling. "Samantha, you remember me, don't you?" Samantha gave her a doggy grin. "Tell Bruiser I'm okay." She didn't want to have to call Mandy, but if the big dog wouldn't let her in the gate, what else could she do? Thankfully, the Husky walked over to the gate and sniffed, then sat down. Bruiser stopped growling and gave a tentative wag of his tail. Then he sat down too. Taking that as a sign he'd accepted her, Amber reached for the gate. Bruiser didn't make a sound. *Okay, that was good, but how do I open the gate, drive the car through and shut the gate again without the dogs getting out on this busy road?* Amber wondered. It was just a two-lane country road, but many cars zipped down it.

Suddenly, Bruiser jumped up and so did Samantha. But instead of heading toward the gate, they turned and ran off in the other direction, barking all the way. Amber quickly pushed the gate open, got in her car and drove through, jumped out, closed the gate and got back in her car. Whew. She didn't know what caught their attention, but at this point she didn't care, just felt grateful they'd been distracted.

When she pulled up to the house, she reached into the backseat of the car, and pulled out her backpack, then opened the trunk and pulling out her suitcase, headed for the house. Without anyone else around, she had time to really look around the house. She unlocked the door, and heard gravel flying behind her. Mindful of Mandy's warning, she stepped aside. The dogs rushed past her and into the house, tongues flapping and proceeded to slurp up the water from their big metallic bowls until there was nothing left. Then they looked at her with, she thought, hopeful expressions on their faces.

"More?" She laughed. "Oh, all right." She dropped the backpack and suitcase onto the floor, picked up the water bowls and headed for the sink in the island located in the middle of the kitchen. She thought of her mom, who would be horrified to see dog dishes in the kitchen and would tell her to get their water from the tub. But she hadn't seen a bathroom yet, and the dogs looked thirsty. "Just this once," she said aloud to herself and the dogs.

She'd just put the bowls back down on the kitchen floor under the wall of glass windows, when she heard her cell phone ring in her backpack.

"Hi Brenda. I'm here."

"I just wanted to make sure you got there okay. Bob and Nancy wanted me to tell you how grateful they are that you agreed to do this. They felt bad about Mandy's accident and frantic that there was no one else to do the job. They said to eat anything you find in the cupboards and they're sending some money to you for more food, since they left the refrigerator bare. Oh, and Blake talked to Carson and he can help move you next weekend, but not this one. I hope that's okay."

"Yeah, that's fine." They talked awhile longer and she'd just disconnected when the phone rang again. This time it was her mom checking on her.

"Honey, are you sure you'll be okay there by yourself?" her mother asked in a worried tone.

Amber laughed. "Mom, I'm used to living alone." Normally reserved by nature like her father, she didn't mind her own company, but her mother didn't understand that—she was just the opposite. "And anyway, I'm not really alone. There are two guard dogs here—well, maybe only one's a guard dog." She looked at Bruiser, ever on the alert, then at Samantha lying on her back with her feet in the air. "And the cats, and the horses, and the cows—"

"Okay, dear, I get your point." Her mother sighed. "I just hope you won't be too lonely is all."

"Mom, that's what texting is for. Don't worry, I'll be fine."

After her mom ended the call, Amber gave herself a tour. It felt a little weird to stay in the home of someone she'd never met. She felt a bit like she was trespassing and she found herself almost tiptoeing around.

"This is silly," she admonished herself. "I have a right to be here," she said aloud. She wondered if the other neighbors knew she was the new caretaker. It would be horrible if they called the police when they saw someone unfamiliar in the house. She shook off that thought.

Her mom once told Amber that she could tell a lot about people by the way they decorated their homes. In that case, she could sure tell that Bob and Nancy liked animals. Small statues of horses, dogs and cats graced the end tables and the coffee table in the sunken living room. When she looked at the titles of the books in the built-in shelves in one corner, she saw books on horses, cows, and chickens. She saw framed photos of their many animals on the walls and entertainment center, instead of family photos, though one photo showed a man on a horse, and another a woman on a horse. She wondered if they were Bob and Nancy.

After she'd given herself a complete tour of the house, found the cozy guestroom with its own bathroom—complete with another moose and bear light fixture over the double sinks—and then put a few of her things away, Amber heard the dogs bark. She hurried through the house and looked out the windows. She saw Mandy getting out of her mom's car at the gate. Feed time already?

After Mandy and her mom drove away and Amber locked the front gate, she walked back to the house, glad the dogs walked with her. It was so quiet out there in the country—really quiet—and dark.

Despite what she'd told her mom, Amber knew she faced a long lonely night ahead in an unfamiliar house.

Chapter Four

The next morning, Amber woke to the sound of her phone alarm, and wondered where she was for a moment. She lay there for awhile until she remembered.. She'd set the alarm the night before knowing she had to get up early to feed. The animals needed to stay on schedule, Mandy emphasized the and must be fed every twelve hours.

One of the many things Mandy didn't tell her when she'd given Brenda and Amber the tour, was that many of the animals required special, prepared foods and medicine. Pills needed to be crushed into powder and mixed into pellets or grain, hay lightly sprinkled with water, mashes made…the instructions seemed endless. Mandy offered to come over and show Amber how to do the morning feeding as well, but Amber told her she could handle it with the instruction sheet someone thoughtfully put in a plastic sleeve—probably so it could be used over and over again. Who could memorize all that needed to be done, since it varied from the morning feed to the night feed?

Amber gingerly lowered her bare feet to the floor. She'd never been in a home that didn't have wall-to-wall carpets, and expected the wood floors to be cold. At least there was a soft throw rug by the bed to step down onto. She probably should have worn socks to bed, she thought ruefully, but the log cabin quilt on the bed looked so warm—and was. However, now she'd have to walk around to open up her suitcase that she'd left on the hope chest at the foot of the bed. Amber braced for the cold, and felt surprised when the floor wasn't cold at all. In fact, it was warm. In-floor heat?

Bruiser and Samantha waited for her at the front door, so she let them out. She didn't know where they'd slept the night before, but hadn't heard a peep out of them. The cats however, were a different story. She'd felt the bed bounce and heard purrs last night and this morning,

As she opened the doors of the barn, Amber heard a soft *hee-hee-hee* sound. One of the horses had its head over the stall's half door and she could see its nose fluttering. Pretty soon the barn was full of animal talk as all of them let her know they were hungry. She placed the feeding instructions on the nearest plastic garbage can, and then began to read them. There was even an order in which they needed to be fed. Then there were water containers to fill.

An hour later, proud that she got the job done, Amber headed back to the house to feed the dogs and cats, and finally, herself. She'd just finished washing her dishes, when Bruiser barked. She looked out the windows and saw a pickup truck at the gate. Who was it? She hadn't unlocked the gate yet that morning. She decided to let Bruiser out to investigate, and see if he knew the driver before she walked out there. When she opened the door, both Bruiser and Samantha rushed out, barking, but she could see that the gate was open and the truck was going through it. Who had a key besides her and the owners? Would the dogs get out onto the road?

It didn't take the dogs long to reach the gate and Amber saw Samantha wag her tail. Bruiser barked a couple more times, but seemed satisfied and trotted after the truck as it pulled up in front of the barn. She'd better investigate. Amber pulled her hoodie off the black wrought iron coat rack and hurried out the door and down the steps.

The tall, rugged, good-looking man who stepped out of the truck must have heard the front door slam shut, as he stopped and looked up, then waited for her to reach him. He wore an open, padded, flannel shirt with sleeves rolled up, over a snug-fitting, long-sleeved Henley-style T-shirt. He had a green John Deere Tractors baseball-type cap on his head, and reddish-brown beard stubble darkened his face.

"I'm Mick Christopher. You must be the new house-sitter," he said when she got within earshot. "Sorry I'm late."

"Who are you? I mean, what are you doing here? And why do you have a key to the gate?"

He looked surprised, as though she should know. "Didn't Mandy tell you? It's probably on the calendar. I'm the farrier. I'm here to trim the horses' hooves."

"Why do you have a key to the gate?"

He sighed. "Because I have a standing appointment here, every eight weeks, and Bob and Nancy can't always be here."

"Do I have to pay you?"

"No, we worked that out before they left. Now, if you don't mind, I need to get started. I have a full day ahead of me. If you'll bring the horses out, I'll get this done and get out of your hair." He jumped down from the truck and walked around to the back where he pulled out some tools and some kind of leather apron-like thing that he strapped on over his jeans. Amber caught herself staring at him, and walked over to the barn and slid the door open.

How was she supposed to "get" the horses? She didn't think she should just let them out of their stalls. She flipped on the light and looked around. Darn. The horses weren't even in their stalls. Evidently they'd finished eating and walked out to the pasture. Now what? She hated to ask him, but she had no clue what to do. Amber stepped outside the barn. "Um…Mick?"

She saw him look down at her. At five-foot-seven inches she was fairly tall, but still he towered a good intimidating nine inches over her.

"Ready?" he asked her. "Bring them out one at a time."

"Uhh, well, the problem is…they aren't in their stalls anymore. They're out there." She waved her hand toward the pasture.

"Uh-huh. I'll wait while you get them, but I'm running behind, so see if you can catch 'em both, but if not, just bring one and you can get the other while I'm working on the first."

"That's the problem. I-I don't know how to catch them."

"Oh, they're pretty easy. Just don't show 'em the halter," he advised.

"Halter?"

Mick stared at her for a moment, and then seemed to make some kind of a decision. "I'll tell you what; I'll show you how to catch them. Follow me." He turned on his heel and strode into the barn, then grabbed some leather pieces with ropes attached, off of a row of hooks on an inner wall. He held them up to her. "This is a halter," he said pointing to the leather piece. "And this is a lead rope." He held up the rope that dangled from a large ring on the halter. He opened the stall door, walked through the wood shavings and out the back, where he stepped down into the mud. He stopped and looked at her feet in running shoes, and shook his head. "You'd better stay here." He walked through the mud in his work boots, holding the halters and ropes behind his back, and when he approached the horses, held something out to them. They both walked up to him and Amber saw Mick put a rope around each horse's neck, then the halter on one—she didn't remember which was Sugar and which was Spice. "Open that gate when I get there, would ya!" Mick yelled and pointed to the left.

Amber realized there must be a gate to the pasture, and hurried out of the barn.

He led the horses through and she shut the gate, then followed Mick and the horses to a fence-like thing—two wooden posts with another round wooden bar horizontally between them—and watched him tie one of the horses to the bar. Then he turned to her and held out the other horse's rope. "Here, take Sugar, will you? Normally I just tie them up to the hitching post, but since you're here, you can hold them. It will be quicker." He pulled an old-fashioned round watch on a chain, out of his pocket and frowned when he looked at it. "Looks like I'll be late for the next appointment too." He walked over to his truck and grabbed some tools. Amber started to follow him, but the other horse, Spice—now she knew who was who—seemed to protest about her taking his buddy away, and let out a big neigh. Mick looked up and said to the horse, "Stay there."

During the whole time, Amber didn't say a word, embarrassed about her lack of knowledge.

"Don't stand in front of the horse; stand to the side. Sugar is pretty good, but Spice might take it into his head to lunge forward," he explained. "And stand on the side opposite from where I'm working," Mick instructed her, then bent down and tapped on the horse's leg with the tool in his hand. Sugar lifted her foot and he pulled it up. Amber saw that it was full of mud. She watched as Mick pulled a smaller tool out of a pocket in his leather apron. It looked like a hook on a handle. He used it to get the mud out of Sugar's foot, then pulled a rag out of another pocket and wiped the mud off the rest of her leg and foot. "You need to clean their feet out at least once a week when they're barefoot," he told Amber."

"Why?" She had to do *that?*

"To keep them from getting thrush, and stone bruises from rocks. Thrush is a very common bacterial infection that occurs in a horse's hoof, in the frog." He must have seen her frown. "When you pick up the horse's foot, you'll see something shaped like a V in the middle. That's the 'frog.' It starts at the heel and goes down into a point toward the toe. A shoe protects their feet."

"Why don't Sugar and Spice wear them?"

"Because it's winter and Bob and Nancy don't ride in the winter…not that they ride much at all. These horses—well, all these animals actually—are more like pasture ornaments to them." He switched to another tool.

"What are you doing with that tool?" Amber didn't mean to delay his work, but she couldn't help asking.

"They're nippers. First I cut off the excess hoof—the new growth—and then I use the rasp and file her hoof, and shape it. Horses' hooves are like our fingernails. They have to be trimmed and filed."

Amber nodded and continued to watch as he did the same on all four of Sugar's feet. Then he straightened up and stretched his back. "Okay, she's done. Tie her up to the hitching post. It's Spice's turn."

"Uhh…" Amber hesitated. "I…I've never…"

"Let me guess. You've never tied up a horse?" He grinned, reached over and took the rope from her hands and led Sugar to the hitching post. There, he swiftly looped the rope around the bar, and yanked on the end of Spice's rope, undoing the knot, then led the horse to Amber, and handed the rope to her.

Amber forgot that she needed to stand to the

side, and he reminded her. She could feel her face flush in embarrassment. Her fingers felt numb and so did her toes from the cold winter air. She hadn't dressed to stand outside in one place. The hoodie she'd pulled on over her long-sleeve shirt definitely didn't keep her warm. Suddenly, she felt the rope slide through her hand as Spice lurched forward. Mick hurried over, grabbed the rope and led the horse back. He jerked on the rope a couple times and spoke to the horse in a firm tone, then handed the rope back to Amber. As soon as the rope touched her hand, she felt a sharp sting and looked down at it.

Mick must have noticed. "Rope burn. You should wear gloves."

"I'll have to get some."

"I have an extra pair in the truck. Remind me to grab them before I leave."

Spice protested twice more, but this time Amber was ready for him and held on tight to the rope, though her hand burned. When Mick finished, he untied Sugar and said, "If you get the gate, I'll put these two back."

Amber just nodded and hurried over to open the gate.

After Mick took off the halters and turned them loose in the pasture, he handed the halters and ropes to Amber. "Will you put these back? But first, could you open the gate up front? I really need to book out of here." When she nodded again, he untied his leather apron, rolled the tools up in it, put them in the back of his truck, and swung up into the cab.

Amber hurriedly walked across the gravel circular drive toward the gate next to the road, but he was already there, waiting in the truck when she got there. Mick handed her a pair of leather gloves out the window. "Nice to meet you, Amber. Take care of that hand."

She walked slowly back to the house, with Bruiser and Samantha at her heels. "What kind of watch dogs are you? Why didn't you growl at him?" she asked them. They just grinned at her—well, Samantha did, but Bruiser's "grin" looked more like a snarl. A small piece of card stock paper fell out of the gloves and floated to the ground. As she reached down to pick it up, she realized it was Mick's business card. On the back he'd written: If you have any problems, call me.

He *was* kinda' cute.

Amber intended to work on her job search, so after she'd peeled off her outer clothes and put on some warmer socks, she picked up her laptop computer and walked down the stairs to the sunken living room and settled into a comfy leather chair near the stove. She'd been delighted to learn it was fueled by propane and not real wood—the "logs" were fake, though the flames were real—and she didn't have to feed it or carry firewood in from somewhere outside in the cold. She lifted the handle on the recliner, put her feet up on the footrest, leaned back and opened up her laptop. Whether because of the early time she got up that morning, or the heat from the stove, she found herself unable to concentrate on the computer screen. Maybe she'd just kick back and relax for awhile. Someone—either Bruiser or Samantha who lay under the dining room table, or the cats on the chairs there—snored.

Bong. Bong. Bong.

Amber woke up with a start. What time was it? She looked at the tall grandfather clock with the pendulum that swung slowly back and forth. Three o'clock? Then she realized her cell phone was ringing. She hastily pushed the chair up and leapt out. By the time she got back up the steps to the dining room table where she'd left it, the ringing stopped. She checked the number, but it didn't look familiar. Then it rang again. "Hello?"

"Hi Amber, it's Mandy. How did you do with the morning feeding?"

Amber felt a little groggy. She yawned. Mandy? Oh yeah. "Oh, everything went fine."

"Great. I forgot to tell you. It should be about time for the shoer to come."

"Mick? Yeah, he came here this morning," Amber replied.

"Isn't he a hunk?" Mandy asked with enthusiasm. "You're so lucky you got to be there."

"Uh, yeah, I guess." *Lucky? Ha. More like embarrassed.*

"All the girls in my 4-H group agree that he's hot." When Amber didn't say more, Mandy continued. "I called to see how you're doing with the feed. It's probably time to throw a couple bales of hay down."

"Throw them down? From where?"

"Oh yeah, I didn't show you the loft, did I?"

"No, I don't think so. I don't remember seeing it. Hey, where is the nearest store?" Amber asked. "I need to get some fresh vegetables and fruit."

"Well, you can either go to town, or I suppose you could go to Arlington. But, I think Stanwood is closer."

"Isn't this Stanwood?"

Mandy laughed. "No, we're in the country. Stanwood is about nine miles north of here.

****

Most of the women Mick met horseshoeing found an excuse to call him on some pretense or another—especially after he'd given them his business card. Not that he thought he was partucularly good-looking or anything. He really didn't know why they sought out his attention, but females had ever since he was a teenager and grew from a guy smaller than his kid sister, to a tall, six-foot-four. That sure made his sister mad. Many of the girls in high school, who claimed to be her friends, actually used her to get to him. When he'd grown muscular from horseshoeing, it appeared to attract women even more.

Oh, he'd grown accustomed to the attention, but he still found it kind of embarrassing. Sure, he'd realized when he took up shoeing for a living, that the majority of his customers would be women. And of course, being surrounded by women wasn't all bad. He'd dated some of them before he decided to continue his education. Now, he had very little time between his job, school and studying.

He didn't know why he felt this instant attraction to Amber. They didn't appear to have much in common. But he found that he admired her. She'd taken on a job she knew nothing about, in order to support herself he supposed. Even though she lacked knowledge about animals—or anything about country life it appeared—to her credit, she seemed to be a pretty good sport about it.

Maybe he just liked the challenge of a female customer who didn't fawn all over him. Hmm, what excuse could he come up with for stopping by to see her again since he wouldn't be going back to trim Sugar and Spice's hooves for another eight weeks? Oh yeah. He grabbed his keys off the table and walked out the door to his truck.

****

Amber couldn't believe how quickly the day passed. She realized she hadn't eaten anything since breakfast and it was almost feeding time for the animals. She searched the cupboards for something to eat and found some of that dried soup that just needed boiling water added to it. She definitely needed to get some fruit and vegetables and other supplies.

After she'd fed the dogs and cats, she headed out to the barn. This time, she put on a warm hat and gloves, and wrapped a knit scarf around her neck. When she stepped out the door, she could see her breath, and shivered.

She fed each pair of animals and Woolie and gave the cows the last of the hay. She gave the horses their oats to eat while she went upstairs to the loft and got down some more bales of hay.

But when she tried to grab the hay, she found there were three strands of orange twine around each large bale and they were tied so tight, she couldn't get her fingers under the twine to pick up the bale. She tried to shove them, but they were too heavy and wouldn't budge. The warm hat she'd put on made her head itch, so she pulled it off. She thought about removing her coat too, she was so warm from straining to move the hay bales, but figured she'd be too cold then. Maybe if she took off the gloves Mick gave her, she could get her fingers under the twine.

"Ouch." A piece of hay sticking out of the twine pricked her skin right on the rope burn, and she still couldn't get a hold of the twine anyway. She felt so frustrated she let herself sink down onto the bale. Then she heard the dogs bark—just a couple half-hearted woofs, though. A few minutes later she heard the sound of someone walking on the gravel driveway. Bruiser came racing into the barn and looked up at her, Samantha not far behind. "Who's here?" she found herself asking—as though they could answer.

"It's me, Mick," came a male voice from

below. "Where are you?"

"Up here. In the loft."

"Getting some hay?"

"Trying to."

"I see some hay hooks on the wall. Do you have some more up there?" Mick asked her.

Hay hooks? "I-I don't know." She heard the sound of boots on the stairs, and soon Mick's head and the rest of him, popped into view. He held something up.

"These are hay hooks," he told her. "Here, I'll get the hay. How many bales do you need?"

"Two, thanks." She stepped aside, and pointed to the hole in the floor above the feed room. "Could you just drop them down there?" When he nodded, she watched as he grabbed either end of the hay bale with a hook and lifted it. Could she do that? "How much do you think those bales weigh?" she asked.

He grunted. "Oh, about 120 pounds, I imagine, with the three strands of twine." He shoved the bale down the hole, then picked up another and did the same. Mandy said he was a hunk, but Amber hadn't paid much attention before and he'd worn the warm, lined outer shirt. Now, he'd stripped down to the Henley, unbuttoned at the collar. It molded to his muscular chest, and strong arms.

"Thanks again," Amber said as she followed him down the stairs. "I couldn't get my fingers around the twine to grab it," she admitted. Once inside the feed room, she saw that one of the bales opened up and broke apart, probably from being dropped on the concrete floor.

"You need a knife like this," Mick told her as he pulled a folded up knife out of his pocket, and proceeded to cut the remaining twine from the bale. "Bob and Nancy must have something around here to open them, though. Ask Mandy."

"I will. Hey, why are you back? Did you leave something behind this morning?"

"I came back to check on my horses."

"*Your* horses?" She raised an eyebrow.

"Yeah, that's what I call all my regular customers." He must have seen the skeptical look on her face, because he grinned. "Actually, I came back to give you something." He walked out of the feed room to an overturned bucket, where he picked up a stack of books. "Here, I brought these for you. I figured you could use them." He held the books out to her. "I don't have any about goats—or sheep. They're not something I'm interested in, but you could probably find something at the Stanwood Library."

She took the three books from him. One was about horses, one about cattle, and one about chickens and turkeys.

Amber didn't know what to think. It was a kind, thoughtful gesture, bringing the books, since she'd just met him. "Thanks."

"Okay, well I'd better get home and feed my horses. I don't know if you've heard the weather reports, but it's supposed to get real cold tonight."

"No, I haven't seen any weather reports lately, thanks." Did she dare ask him if she needed to do something special to be ready for cold weather—and show more of her ignorance? No thanks." Instead, she asked, "You have horses?"

"Yeah, three mustangs. One's not rideable yet, but his mother is. And Buck, I got when he was a three-year-old. He was captured in Oregon. He's the reason I got the other two."

Amber wanted to ask him more, but she heard the impatient stomping of hooves. "Well thanks again, Mick—for everything. I'd better get back to feeding."

"Sure. See ya." He waved his hand and Amber watched him walk to the gate where he'd parked his truck. No wonder she hadn't heard him. He'd left his big noisy diesel pickup parked in front of the gate next to the road. Before he could catch her watching him, she turned and walked back into the barn to give the horses their hay.

By the time Amber got back to the house, she felt really cold. She fed the dogs and cats and found another package of dry soup in the cupboards and some crackers to go with it. While she waited for the soup to stand for three minutes, she decided something hot to drink might help her get warmer too. She wasn't much of a tea drinker, but her mom often drank it, so when she couldn't find any cocoa in the cupboards, she settled for that. At least the cup of tea and the container of soup felt good on her hands when she carried them to the table.

After she'd eaten the soup and washed the

spoon and mug, she walked down to the living room, curled up on a sofa and opened up her laptop. The warmth from the stove felt good, but she could feel a draft from somewhere, so she grabbed a blanket off another sofa and wrapped it around her shoulders. Shortly after that, the tabby cat, Zee, climbed onto her shoulder and purred in her face, then the black cat, Shadow, walked across the keyboard and curled up on her lap. "You guys must be cold too, huh?" she asked them. Then she laughed. Her friends would laugh too if they knew she'd begun to carry on regular conversations with animals.

Chapter Five

Amber woke up some time during the night—or maybe it was early morning—shivering. She couldn't seem to get warm. She got out of bed and searched for a linen closet, hoping to find an extra blanket inside. Aha. Found it. She pulled a blanket out of the closet and took it back to the guest room. The blanket did the trick and she soon drifted off to sleep.

Amber looked out the window while she dressed the next morning and was surprised to see that the ground looked all white. No wonder she'd felt so cold. It must have got down to freezing the night before. When she opened the door to go out, a blast of cold air hit her in the face.

"Brrr." She shivered again and hoped she could hurry through the feeding and get back inside the house, but everything seemed to take longer than usual. She found it hard to do much with gloves on, so she pulled them off. Finally, the only thing left to do was fill the water containers and dishes and check the water troughs. She walked outside to the faucet and pulled the hose off the reel until it reached the water trough in the corral, went back to turn the water on, and then back again to the trough. To her surprise, the water in the trough was frozen. She pushed on it with her fingers, but it didn't budge or even crack. Hmm. She opened the gate to the corral and walked through, latching it behind her. She pushed on the ice again, but it still wouldn't budge. Maybe a rock? But when she looked around, the only rocks she saw were too small and frozen to the ground. What should she do? Then she had an idea.

Amber half-sat on the edge of the metal water tub, and holding her leg up, plunged it down with all her might. Her foot finally broke through the water. Of course, her shoe and socks and foot were all wet and really cold now, but at least there was some water. Still, she needed to add more. The horses and cows drank a lot of water after they had hay, she'd noticed. But why didn't any water come out of the hose? Now what should she do? Maybe it would warm up and she could fill the trough up later.

After she broke the frozen water in the goats' dish and the chickens' and saw that they didn't have enough, she walked back to the house. Amber searched through the cupboards and found a big pot. She put it in the sink and ran some water, then decided she should make it warm water and waited for what seemed like an eternity for the cold water to turn to warm.

When she picked the pot up out of the sink, she could barely move it. She dumped half the water out, and then struggled to open the door and go back outside. Half the pot wasn't enough for the goats and chickens, and she ended up making two more trips back and forth. She also added some to the water trough, hoping it would help melt the ice there.

Amber just wanted to collapse by the stove

and warm her hands and feet, but the cats wound themselves around her legs, wanting to be fed, and Samantha and Bruiser stared at her with accusing eyes. "Okay, okay, I get it," she said to the four of them.

Around noon, Mandy called. "My mom said I should call on my lunch break and see how you're doing with the animals in this weather. It sure was cold when I fed our horses this morning."

"Yeah, especially with the frozen trough, water buckets and the hose."

"Oh, I guess I forgot to tell you to put the water heaters in."

"Water heaters?"

"Yeah, they're hanging up on a wall in the feed room. You just drop them in the water trough and plug them into the orange extension cord and they keep the water from freezing."

"What about the hose?"

"Did you shake the water out the last time you rolled it up?" the girl asked.

"I don't know. I wound the crank and it rolled itself up onto the holder thingy. Am I supposed to do something else?"

"In the winter, you just want to make sure you get all of the water out of the hose each time you use it."

"Ohhh. I didn't know that. I will from now on, though. Thanks for the tip, Mandy," she said, thinking that now she had one more thing to add to the daily chores.

"Where can I get some work boots? Which department store do you have here?"

Mandy laughed. "I wish. None. Your best bet is the feed store."

"Is the library right in town?" Amber asked.

"Oh, do you like to read? I don't."

"I don't usually have time when I'm working but now, well, I have a lot of time. Mick brought some books for me about horses and cows and chickens, but I thought I'd get one on goats. He said—"

"Mick brought you books?"

"You seem surprised."

"Well, he's a nice guy and all. I mean, he did come and talk to my 4-H group when I asked him, but he didn't stick around afterward and he's always in a hurry when he comes out to shoe our horses. Mom's offered him a soda on hot days and hot chocolate on cold ones, but he always turns her down."

"Maybe he needs to get to his next appointment. He was in a big hurry when he came out for Sugar and Spice."

"Come to think of it, he's always late."

Just before three, Amber said goodbye to Bruiser and Samantha at the front gate. "Be a good boy, Bruiser. Try to keep him in line, Sammy." She patted their soft, furry heads, then got back into her car and looked at the GPS on her phone. She'd searched for the address of the feed store and then put it in her GPS.

Even though the sun was out, some places on the road were shaded and Amber felt the tires slip a little. She tensed up. She usually didn't drive on icy days, she rode the bus. The drive down the road was fairly dark with all the trees on either side, but suddenly one side opened up and Amber briefly turned her head to see why. She saw water and then land beyond that. She wished she didn't have to drive so she could really look around, but she needed to concentrate on her driving.

When she reached the small town, she thought it might be fun to walk up and down the streets, look in the windows and go inside any of the stores that interested her on the main street. It would be more fun to go with someone, though—maybe when her family came up for a visit—and she needed to get to the feed store before it closed.

She pulled up in front of a large concrete building that looked like a grocery store.

"This is a feed store?" she said aloud, but sure enough she saw a large sign across the double glass doors. She sat in the car for a moment, still a little shaky from the drive. Then she grabbed her purse off the passenger seat, got out of her car and began to cross the parking lot.

"Amber!" someone shouted. She looked around. "Over here." Mick stood at the entrance to the store and held the door open.

Amber scurried across the lot, and through the open door. "Thanks," she said.

"Are you here to buy some feed?" Mick asked her.

"No, actually I need some boots. Mandy suggested I get them here."

"Yeah, this is the best place in town to do that. Half of it used to be a clothing store, but it went out of business and the feed store expanded and added western and work clothes."

"How about you?"

"I already have boots." He laughed. "But I'd be willing to help you find some."

"No, silly—"she punched him lightly on the arm like she did with her brothers when they teased—"I know you have boots. I meant, what are you doing here?"

"I have to get some grain and a new feed dish for my horses. Buck chewed up the last one. He's still a colt at heart."

When they walked farther into the store, Amber looked around in awe. "My friend Brenda would love this place. I see all kinds of horse stuff."

"Not just horse, but chickens and dogs and cats and rabbits and gardening things…and the clothes are over here. You want to look around or just go right to the boots?"

"I'd better just go look at boots." She wasn't sure how much she could afford. She still hadn't received her last paycheck from McNeil, Harrison and Taylor. She'd called them back and they said it would be right out. She hoped it would be there when she went to Seattle. She needed to buy some groceries and hoped she had enough to cover everything. At this rate, she'd have to cash out her retirement account—the little amount she'd accrued since she finally became eligible.

But it was not to be. The boots cost more than she'd anticipated. She'd also seen a tall pair of black cowboy boots, she could wear anywhere. She stared at them with longing

"Couldn't you find any boots that fit?" Mick asked when he walked up.

"No. I'd better go to the grocery store. I need to get back and feed."

"How about these?" Mick held up a pair of bright pink rubber boots, his eyes glinting with amusement.

"Are you kidding? Those look like something my five-year-old nephew's girlfriend would wear."

"He has a girlfriend? Hmm."

She made a face at him. "I don't know, but if he did...what I'm saying is, those are for kids."

Then she saw the smirk on his face, and lunged for him, but he neatly side-stepped and grabbed up another pair of boots.

"Why don't you try these on?"

She wondered if he was serious or not, but the blue boots looked to be her size. She couldn't afford them, but didn't want to say it, so she decided to humor him. "Okay. Is there a place to sit down?" She looked around.

"I don't see anything. Here"—he held out an arm—"grab onto me with one hand and shove your foot in the boot with the other."

She hesitated. "No, that's not necessary," she

protested. "I'll—"

"Amber, I won't let you fall. You can trust me."

"Oh, all right." She grabbed onto his strong arm. The contact jolted her as if she'd touched the hot wire on an electric fence. She tried to conceal her reaction, and let him steady her. The boot slipped on easily and unfortunately, it fit.

"You just slip that loop there over the button and it will keep them from coming off in the mud." Mick still steadied her with one hand, leaned down and with his other hand, pulled the loop over for her. "Like this." He straightened up. "What do you think? They look like a perfect fit to me."

Amber sighed. "No, I think I'll have to come back another day. I need to—"

Mick leaned close to her and whispered, "If you don't have the money, don't worry. I'll get 'em for you."

"I can't let you do that," Amber protested.

"Yes you can. You can pay me back someday, if you must. But, by the looks of the sky out there, you'll need them soon. It looks like a snow sky."

"Really? Well okay, I guess I'd better get them then," she said with reluctance. "But it's just a loan until I get paid," Amber hastily assured him.

Mick carried the boots over to the checkout counter and paid for them, then carried them out to her car. "There you go," he said as he put them in the trunk. Then they just stood there awhile, not saying anything, so she opened the door and got into the driver's seat.

"Well, thanks again, for the loan. I guess I should go now. I need to go to the store and"—Amber looked down at the gas gauge—"get some gas. Can you point me in the right direction?"

"There's only one grocery store, but it has a gas station too. I could show you where it is," he offered.

"I don't want to keep you any longer. Don't you need to get your grain and bucket?"

"Yeah, I should. Well, you take care, Amber," Mick said and reached out to push a stray lock out of her eyes, then paused as though he wanted to say something, but then turned away.

Amber waited another minute and watched him walk to his truck. Something about him appealed to her, but she didn't know why. He was obviously a country boy, and she was a city girl. What could they possibly have in common? But still, she found herself attracted to him...and for a moment there she thought he looked as though he might kiss her. She hoped she'd get paid soon so she'd have an excuse to see him again. She started the car.

She tried to hurry, first at the gas station and then at the grocery store. She could see the sky darkening and figured she would get back just in time to feed. She was appalled at the price of the food and that it took every bit of the rest of her cash to get just a few vegetables and some fruit. Again, she wished she'd get paid soon. Then she remembered her employment checks would go to her apartment. She really needed to go home and check her mailbox. It would be good to go back to Seattle for awhile. She missed city life. Maybe she could meet a friend for lunch while she was there.

Amber turned into the driveway, and before she opened the gate, she checked the mailbox. She felt surprised to see an envelope with her name on it. She slit it open with her fingernails, and noticed that she'd broken another nail. Maybe she should just cut them off since they kept breaking. Inside the envelope, she found a check and a short note. It was from Nancy, who wrote to thank her for helping them out on such short notice, and that the check was half her pay in advance and some extra for the food she'd have to buy in order to make up for the bare refrigerator. She looked at the amount. If only she'd had this earlier, she wouldn't have needed to take Mick's money. But now she could pay him back. She shoved the check back into the envelope and got back in the car, but not before she petted Samantha and cooed at Bruiser who gave her only one growl before he slowly wagged his tail. Progress.

Amber hurriedly put the food in the refrigerator that needed to be kept cold, unloaded the other bag and put things away. Then she sat down and exchanged her running shoes for the rubber boots, and grabbing the gloves off the table, she headed back outside with the dogs trailing behind.

Thank goodness she'd had the sense to put the heater in the water trough when Mandy told her about it, as the sun came out briefly and warmed things up during the day. She'd also tested the hose and found that it warmed up enough to thaw, so she filled up all the water buckets and the trough. This time, before she rolled the hose up, she shook it until the water stopped coming out, and for good measure, in case it wasn't a freeze-proof faucet, she unhooked the hose from the faucet as well.

It seemed even colder than that morning, and Amber hurried through her chores as quickly as possible.

When she got inside, she pulled out her cell phone and the card Mick had given her and dialed his number. The phone picked up quickly and went right to voicemail. She hadn't called a man in a long time, and felt almost glad she didn't reach him in person. After stumbling over her words a bit, she told him she got paid and wanted to reimburse him for the boots, gave him her cell phone number, and ended the call.

After a dinner that included steamed vegetables and fresh fruit, she washed up her dishes and settled on a sofa with a blanket over her, and called her parents' number.

"Hello?" Brenda answered.

"Oh, you're there. Good."

"Hi Amber. Hey everybody, its Amber. How are you? We heard it got pretty cold there this morning."

"It sure did. And now I've heard it might snow. I hope not; I want to come home for awhile." She talked to Brenda a bit longer, and then to Blake and then her mom, but they were just about to sit down to dinner, so she ended the call, opened up her laptop and logged onto her Facebook page. Her days started so early now, that soon staring at the screen made her tired, and she logged off of the computer. Hmm. Mick hadn't called her back yet. Where could he be this late at night? None of her business, she reminded herself. Maybe she should read one of the books he'd brought.

With a start, Amber realized she'd fallen asleep. She picked the book up off the floor where it must have fallen when she dozed off. When she stood in the doorway, waiting for the dogs to come back in, she didn't see any snow coming down. Still, it was cold and after she got in bed, she felt glad for their warmth after Zee and Shadow jumped up and curled up in their usual spots.

Chapter Six

The first thing Amber noticed when she woke up the next morning, was the extreme quiet. It was actually fairly quiet there most of the time, although occasionally the bull a couple fields over let out a bellow. And sometimes the narrow two-lane country road that ran past the property could be noisy. She supposed it was because it was a straight stretch of road from the top of the hill past the house and on for quite awhile, because she'd actually seen two cars racing each other. After that, she was extra careful to make sure the dogs didn't get out the gate when she or anyone else drove through.

But this morning, it was eerily quiet. She sat up and pulled the curtains aside. Oh no. The weatherman was right. Snow. She was so glad she'd accepted Mick's offer to pay for the boots instead of waiting until she could afford them.

Amber got up and walked out to the dining room where the dogs slept under the table. They crawled out and headed for the door. When she opened it to let them out, she felt appalled to see how much snow covered the ground and everything else. It must be six inches deep. She wouldn't be driving anywhere.

She was about to shut the door, when some movement caught her eye. Samantha looked to be totally in her element. She put her nose down and scooted along the ground until she flopped down and rolled back and forth, from side to side, in the snow. Amber laughed. "Are you making snow angels, Sammy?" The dog jumped up, and shook, snow flying everywhere. Then the Husky snuffled and snorted, and turned to look at Amber with a big smile on her face. Bruiser did a bit of rolling too, but quickly jumped back up and ran to the fence, barking. Amber looked and saw Sugar and Spice running around the pasture, kicking up their heels. Even the cows, Heidi and Gretchen, got caught up in the excitement, as they ran a short distance too, which made Bruiser bark even more and race up and down the fence.

"You'd like to herd them, wouldn't you boy?" Amber called to him. "After all, you are a German *Shepherd*. You need a job, huh?"

Amber shut the door and walked back to the guest room to get dressed. She put on two pair of socks—she really should have brought some thicker ones, another thing to add to her list of things she needed to buy—two shirts and a sweater, leggings and jeans, a hat and a scarf, and her work gloves. Then she ventured outside...and slipped down the steps, face-first into the snow.

Soon she felt a warm wet tongue slurping her face and looked up to see two furry heads with brown eyes staring at her...and then Bruiser shook and covered her with wet drops of snow.

"Thanks," she said to the dog. She couldn't help laughing, though her knee hurt. She rolled over to her back and lay there for a few minutes, until the cold started to seep through her clothing. Then she struggled to sit up. Gosh, her knee really hurt. She must have hit it on something when she landed. She sat there and wondered how she could get up onto her feet.

Plop.

A snowball landed next to her. She looked up, and saw Mick. Did he see her fall? She felt embarrassed enough that he saw her there on the ground.

"You didn't hear me, did you? I called your name," Mick said as he walked up.

"My ears must be full of snow," she replied, wondering why Bruiser didn't bark. Maybe he'd been distracted at the sight of her on the ground—even though it wasn't his fault this time.

"Here, let me help you get up." Mick reached down.

"I think I've hurt my knee. I must have landed on it or something," she told him.

"Let me look. Take my hand."

After a moment's hesitation, she took his extended hand and then attempted to put her full weight on her right leg. It hurt, but she figured she could walk.

"Thanks," she said. She was all too aware of the warmth of his work-roughened hand and its effect on her again. His grip felt strong. It seemed as though he held onto her a little longer than necessary too. When he let go, she brushed the snow off her clothes. "Those stairs are slippery," she said to explain her fall. Still embarrassed, she changed the subject. "Did you get my message?"

"Yeah, but it was too late to call when I got home, so I decided to drive over. When I walked up, I saw you lying on the ground. I'm glad to see you're alive and well." He grinned. "You are okay, right?"

"I'm okay." Even if she wasn't, she wouldn't admit it; she didn't want him to think she was totally inept. She gritted her teeth and took a step forward. Not too bad...*Yikes*. Pain shot through her knee. She wobbled a little, but took another step.

Are you sure you're okay?" Mick asked.

She was so busy trying to concentrate that she barely paid attention to what he said. "Sorry, what?"

"You don't look okay. Looks like you can hardly walk," he said to her in a doubtful tone of voice. "I'd better feed the outdoor animals for you this morning. You should go back in and ice that knee."

Determined not to be a wuss, Amber continued to walk toward the barn, and tried not to limp too bad. She waved a hand at him. "I'm fine."

"I'm not working today. There isn't much call for shoeing when it snows like this. Hey, feeding will go twice as fast if I help."

"Well, if you really want to, thanks." She'd be able to spend more time with him...Stop it. Remember? Country boy...city girl? she argued with herself as she hobbled off to the door, which took longer than it normally did, in the deep snow. Before she could get the door rolled open on its track, she heard the calls of hungry animals in the barn. She felt bad that she couldn't move very fast and because she knew the animals wanted their breakfast *now*. But each step she took on her injured knee felt painful.

Mick scooped up the chicken feed into a big coffee can and headed out to their pen. When he came back in he asked, "Where's the straw? The chickens need some in their coop to keep the cold out." He looked around.

Amber looked around too. She hated to admit once again that she didn't have a clue, but what the heck, she just wanted to get the feeding over and go back in the house. Her fingers felt frozen in the work gloves. "Uhh…"

"Looks like hay but more of a yellowish color. No green. Big stalks," Mick prompted her.

She shook her head. "No, I don't think there's any here."

"Maybe you need to make another trip to the feed store. Need anything else there?" When she just looked at him, he said, "I'll look around. Do you have enough shavings for the stalls?" he asked.

"Um…"

"I'll look for those too." He nodded and then walked into the feed room, and called out, "Looks as though you're getting low on grain too. Better get a bag or two."

Amber wondered if her check from Bob and Nancy would cover everything plus pay Mick back for the boots. But first, she needed to go to the bank and cash the check. "Um, Mick?"

He stuck his head out of the feed room. "Yeah?"

"Can I get a ride into town with you? I need to go to the bank and cash the check I just got. Then I could pay you back and get the things I need at the feed store."

"Yeah, I could do that, but I'll tell you what. I'll give you ride into town…for a kiss."

"What?"

"You heard me." There was a devilish twinkle in Mick's eyes and he took a step closer. "I like you, Amber, and I think you like me. What have you got to lose? Just one little kiss."

"Uhh…" Gee, this guy moved fast. But what the heck? She nodded. "Well, okay."

He cupped her cheek and dropped his head. His lips touched hers in a kiss so gentle her head felt light. It ended too soon.

He stepped back.

"There now, that wasn't too bad was it?"

"No." What she really wanted to say was, 'Are you kidding? That was amazing.'

"Why don't you grab an ice pack or a bag of frozen peas and we can ice your knee on the drive into town?"

"I will when we get back." For now, she just wanted to think about his kiss.

She didn't know if he heard her, because he continued to look around the barn, then walked out a side door. "Oh, here are the shavings. Looks like plenty. How often do you clean the stalls?"

Oh no, one more thing Mandy didn't tell her.

Amber left the dogs in the house. She thought it might be too cold for them to be out, though probably with their thick coats, they'd be fine. Then she walked slowly across the driveway to where Mick warmed up the truck. She wished she could have taken the time to ice her knee, but didn't think she should ask Mick to wait when he was kind enough to take her. Her clothes felt tight around her knee, so she assumed it must be swollen. It sure hurt enough.

She opened the door of the pickup to a blast of welcome heat. But when she put the foot of her uninjured leg up on the chrome running board, her boot slipped on the packed snow on it. Should she put her bad leg up first? It was quite a step up to the cab of the four-wheel drive vehicle. The truck seemed higher off the ground than most pickups—not that she'd had much experience with trucks; everyone she knew drove a car. She reached up and grabbed the handhold inside the truck and tried again to pull herself up, vaguely aware of the sound of boots crunching in the snow. Next thing she knew, strong arms lifted her up until she was inside the truck and on the seat. She sat there, stunned for a moment, then, with a flushed face, searched for the shoulder harness and seatbelt…and couldn't find it.

Mick spoke from the driver's side, "They get stuck between the seats sometimes. Here, I'll get it." He leaned across her and pulled the buried belt out, and a frisson of sensation passed through her—

something she hadn't felt for a long time—when she felt his warm breath on her face.

When he got the seatbelt fastened, Mick grabbed the gearshift on the floor. "I need to put it into four-wheel drive," he told her. The pickup lurched onto the snowy road, which made Amber grab the handhold with her right hand and the shoulder portion of her seatbelt in her left. Mick looked over at her and grinned. "Nervous?"

"A little. I'm nervous about the snow," she hastened to add lest he think she might be scared of his driving.

"Uh-huh." He was quiet for a moment until they came to a pasture full of cows and a few horses, with a dilapidated, weathered barn. "Did you know they filmed a movie here once?"

"Well no, no one told me that before. What was it called?" If a movie had been filmed there, she couldn't tell by looking at it. She didn't notice anything spectacular about the place, although since it was at the top of a steep hill, coming in the other direction from town, it might have a good view.

"Uh…oh yeah, 'The Ring.' They built a cabin down in that gully, and there was a fake bright orange tree in the pasture."

"That's cool. I remember that movie," Amber told him.

"So, what do you do when you're not house-sitting? Or is that what you do for a living?" Mick turned to face her. Amber wished he'd keep his eyes on the road.

"No, actually this is my first house-pet-sitting

job. I'm a paralegal. Well, I was," she amended. "I got laid off recently."

"Where did you work?" he asked. At least he'd turned back to face the road, she noted, probably because he had to—it was hard to tell where the road was in many places. The divider line between the lanes was covered with deep snow as well as the shoulder boundaries, and it didn't look as though anyone else had ventured out yet. She didn't see any tracks in the snow.

"I worked in downtown Seattle in a high-rise building for a large law firm," she answered.

"Do you live in Seattle?" He turned back to face her again.

"Yeah, although I grew up in Bellevue." She decided to turn the conversation back on him. "How about you? Where are you from?"

"Granite Falls."

"So what made you decide to be a-a"—she struggled to remember the name—"farrier?"

"My family always had horses because of my mom. My sister and I were in 4-H and stuff. When I got older and wanted to buy a truck, I decided I could make money shoeing horses. So I studied with an older guy who shod our family horses. But it isn't something I want to do forever."

"Really? How come? What do you want to do?"

"It's hard work which is okay, but it's hard on the body too—especially when I have to deal with horses who want to kill me—and I can't see doing it for the rest of my life. I'm taking a mostly online college program in business." He fell silent for a moment. "Have you ever thought of working for a small firm, maybe in a small town? They have lawyers in this town, you know."

"I don't know if I want to stay in the legal field…" she trailed off.

"Do you like what you do?"

"I did."

"Well then maybe it's the place you didn't like and not the job itself."

"Maybe." She turned her head to look out the window. "Look!" she exclaimed and pointed. "What is that big bird standing in that pasture? It's a blue-gray color with long legs.

Mick must have turned to look. "It's a blue heron. You'll see them by the water and in the fields."

When they reached the area where they left the trees and the road opened up, she asked, "What is that water down there?"

"Oh, that's Puget Sound and Camano Island."

Amber looked briefly out the window again. "Wow, look at all those seagulls. There must be hundreds out in that farmer's field," she commented, noticing the white birds that nearly covered the land from the farmhouse to the edge of the water.

Mick laughed. "Actually, those are snow geese, and there are probably ten thousand of them. They come here from Siberia every year."

"That is so cool. I've never seen anything like it." She stared at the large birds.

"Where do you want to go first?" Mick

asked, jolting Amber out of her thoughts.

"I'd better get to the bank before it closes, and then I can pay you back the money I borrowed."

"It's no big deal. I can wait," he told her.

"No, I want to do it now. I don't like to owe anybody," she insisted.

They reached town shortly after that and Mick drove her to the bank where Amber cashed the check— she'd decided she should keep cash on hand rather than deposit it in the bank. Then Mick took them down the main street to the feed store. Amber decided she liked sitting up high in a truck as she got a better view of the town. It seemed to be made up of mostly antique stores and specialty shops, a bookstore, a couple dentist offices, the police department, a tavern, a funeral home, and a café. They'd passed a large chain drugstore and a restaurant on the way to the bank. She didn't want to insult him, but she didn't think there was much to the town. "No fast food joints here?" she asked him. There were several empty stores. She wondered why.

"It's a typical small town these days. The grocery stores and fast food places and lots of other businesses are in strip malls as you head out of town. If we'd come in off the freeway instead of the back road, you'd have seen a lot more stores and the cinema and fast food places, and the high school. But there are a couple cafes in town and the library—"

"The library? I wondered where it was."

"Are you a reader? I have to read so many

textbooks right now I don't feel like reading anything else. Have you read the books I brought?"

She didn't want to tell him the truth: she felt so tired after the early mornings and all the physical labor of feeding the outdoor animals, she practically fell into bed every night, or fell asleep in the chair when she started to read. "Some, but I also want to get a book on goats. When the snow's gone, I'll come back into town."

"That might be awhile. When the snow melts, we'll probably have flooding," Mick told her.

"Are you kidding me?"

"No, it usually floods a couple times a year around here," he said nonchalantly as he pulled the big pickup into the parking lot.

"Maybe Bob really *is* Noah," Amber muttered to herself. Mick must have heard her. He laughed.

After they'd ordered and paid for what they needed, they walked back out to the truck. Mick helped her climb back up into it again and then drove over to the loading dock where the bale of straw, sacks of grain for her and sacks of feed he bought, were loaded into the back of the pickup.

"Would you like to see a little bit more of the town?" Mick asked as they pulled out of the lot.

"Sure, if you have time."

Instead of taking the same road back that they came in on, Mick turned right at the light by the drugstore. "This is the Stanwood-Camano highway which, of course, goes to Camano Island," he told her. "And there's 'Johnny's'. They have great pizzas and other Italian food. It's always packed. In the summer, I swear I can smell the pizza a mile away."

Amber didn't see any cars in the lot. "Oh, looks like it's closed now." She realized she felt a little disappointed. She'd thought about taking him to lunch for all the help he'd given her.

"Yeah, but they'll probably be open for dinner." He paused and looked at her. "Would you like to go there for pizza?"

It took a while for his question to register in her brain. Was he asking her out? How should she answer his question in case he wasn't? She must have been silent too long, as Mick spoke again before she could answer.

"I thought you might like to get out. Sometimes a person gets tired of their own cooking. I know *I* do."

It sounded as though he was asking her out. "Tonight?"

"Or some other time if you want," he answered.

"Uh, no...I mean, tonight would be good. I'll buy." When he started to protest, she held up her hand. "I was going to take you to lunch for all the help you've given me."

When they arrived at the gate, Amber unhooked her seatbelt to get out and open it.

"I'll get it," Mick said and got out of the truck before she could even hand him the key. She shook her head; she'd forgotten he had his own key. So she waited in the warmth of the cab while she watched Mick's breath plume out in the cold air.

When he got back in, he drove as close as possible to the house, then came around, opened the passenger door and held out his hand to help her down. "You should go in and ice your knee. I'll put the feed in the barn and some straw in the coop."

"Thanks for all your help." He just nodded, so she carefully walked up the wide steps to the deck and then gingerly across it to the front door.

Bruiser and Samantha waited for her right behind the door. She could hear them whine, but she didn't dare let them out while the front gate was still open. She managed to squeeze through the partially open door and then gave them pets. "Good dogs," she told them. "I'll let you out pretty soon." She limped down the hall to the linen closet, grabbed a washcloth, limped back to the kitchen and peered into the freezer for some ice. Even better, she found an icepack. She sank slowly onto a dining room chair, and placed the icepack over her knee. She could barely feel the cold and decided she needed to take off her jeans. That seemed to work better. She could feel the cold through her leggings.

The dogs dropped down on the floor next to her—Bruiser with his usual *oomph* as he landed hard on the carpet—and stared at her. She wondered how long it would take Mick to do everything he mentioned. She felt bad about not letting the dogs out. Zee came up and rubbed against her leg and purred. She leaned over to pet the striped cat and Shadow appeared, yawning and stretching, and wanted to be petted too. Samantha must have decided she needed attention as well, and waving her bushy tail, she walked over and slurped Amber's face. Not to be outdone, Bruiser jumped up and joined her.

Amber laughed and managed to pet all four of them, but Bruiser kept butting in and pushing against her knee. She tried to push him back, but he must have thought it was a game, and hopped around and barked."

At the same time she felt a draft of cold air, she looked up to see Mick standing in the entryway, laughing. "How's your knee? Did the ice help?" he asked as he petted both dogs, who left her to greet him.

"Yeah, it's much better, thanks."

"Well, I just wanted you to know I finished." and I'm leaving now."

"Do you think you're up to feeding tonight, or should I come back and do it for you?"

"I can do it. Listen, Mick, I—"

"Do you want to go to dinner at Johnny's afterward? About five-thirty?"

"Um, sure. Five-thirty will be fine. Let me give you my cell phone number in case anything comes up."

"I'll be here," he replied, but she'd already written it out along with her name on a napkin—the only thing handy—and held it out to him, so he had no choice but to take it. "See you soon." He started to turn away, but then stopped. "And Amber?"

"Yes?"

"It was my idea to go out to dinner. I'll pay."

She opened her mouth to protest, but he'd

reached down and petted the dogs again, then opened the door and walked out.

    She smiled. Sure seemed like a date to her.

Chapter Seven

Amber hadn't brought any nice, going-out-type clothes with her. She didn't think she'd need them. She spent half an hour trying on outfits and discarding them, before she finally settled on a black turtleneck sweater and wine-colored corduroys, mainly for warmth. As she changed back into her jeans to go outside again, Amber caught a fingernail on the sweater. Shoot. Another broken nail. Her once long, manicured, polished fingernails were now dirty and jagged. She pulled some clippers and a file out of her purse. As she cut them all short, she realized that she'd forgotten about her aches and pains from the fall, and in fact, her knee felt much better.

When Mick arrived, he drove all the way up to the house again and insisted on helping her up into the truck. She decided not to tell him she could have done it herself now.

Surprisingly the air felt warmer, and as they rode along, she saw evidence of the snow melting in the fields and on buildings and parked vehicles. The roads were slushy, but slippery. Amber felt impressed by Mick's driving skills, but didn't say anything to him about it. She supposed everyone in the country was used to driving in the snow and was afraid he'd only think less of her, a city girl.

Still, the snow was deep, and Amber felt surprised to see so many vehicles in the parking lot when they pulled up at Johnny's. But then she looked around and saw that most of them seemed to be four-wheel drive like Mick's truck. "Looks crowded," she said to him.

"Yeah, it always is on a Saturday night," he replied. "There aren't a lot of choices in fine-dining around here." He swept his arm around as if to encompass the town. "The choices are Mexican, Chinese or Italian—that's Johnny's. They have the best food."

When they reached the double doors to the restaurant, Amber could see through the golden glass panes that a crowd of people stood in the entryway, and when Mick opened a door for her, she saw more people seated on the wooden benches on either side of the entrance. She turned and looked at Mick to see if he wanted to leave, but he grasped her arm and gently moved her forward. "Next time, we'll have to come during the week when it isn't so crowded, "Mick murmured in her ear from where he stood close behind her.

Next time? "Hmmm. Something smells good."

"It's the pizza."

Amber noted with relief, that a large part of the crowd waiting in line were led away to some long tables on the other side of the room. When the hostess walked up and asked how many in their party, Mick answered, "Two" and she beckoned for them to follow her to a small table. Several people said "hi" to Mick and nodded at her as they made their way to the table, and Amber couldn't help notice that several women ogled him too.

After they'd studied the menus for awhile, Mick asked Amber what she wanted.

"What do you suggest since I've never been here until tonight?"

"Everything's good, however, my suggestion is the pizza. It's really good." He smiled and she noticed for the first time that he'd shaved the stubble from his face. Who knew that under the beard was a cute dimpled chin? She needed to stop staring at him.

"Pizza sounds good to me," she responded. She'd thought about ordering the spaghetti, but then realized how messy that could be, and kind of embarrassing on a first date. Was this a first date…or an only date?

The waitress came and took their order, then returned with the house salads and warm bread. Amber didn't realize she was so hungry and felt surprised when she looked down at her empty plate. Of course, she'd become accustomed to eating a lot earlier than this, since she fed the animals and went to bed early.

When she looked up, she saw Mick staring at her. "What? Do I have something on my chin?" she asked. Oh why did she say 'chin'? She'd meant to say 'face.'

"I enjoy watching you eat. Most women I've dated just pick at their food."

Amber felt her face grow warm. "I didn't eat

much today." How many women had he gone out with?

"Hope you have room for the pizza." He grinned at her.

"Hey, Mick, how are ya?" A thirty-something blonde in tall rubber boots stopped at their table, with a check in her hand. Two other women in boots and jeans stood behind her. "Here's that money I owe you for the other day." She held the check out to him.

"Oh, thanks Mardie. Hey Sue, Diane." He looked past Mardie at the taller blonde, and a brunette.

"Hey, Mick," the one named Sue said. "I just got a new colt. You've gotta see him. He's a Kiger from Oregon. He looks a lot like your Buck."

Amber felt a little uncomfortable as the three women and Mick discussed horses. But Mick suddenly stopped talking and turned to her. "This is Amber Preston. She's staying at Bob and Nancy's place." The three women nodded at her.

"Has Spice done his rope trick for you yet?" the tall blonde named Diane, asked her and then laughed.

Amber looked across the table at Mick, but he appeared to be waiting for her answer too. "I don't think so. What does he do?" she asked curiously.

"He twirls a twig in his mouth like he's twirling a lasso. He's an old ranch horse from Montana," Mick explained.

"Yeah, it's a hoot," Mardie said with a smile.

"Bob needs to get a video of it." The three women chatted a little longer, but when the waitress walked up to their table with a large silver tray, Mardie observed, "Well, looks like your food's here. We'd better let you eat your dinner. Come on, girls."

"See ya, Mick," each of them said as they left.

Amber felt surprised to realize she was glad to see them go. Could she be feeling possessive of Mick? The women all knew him a lot longer than she did. They were his customers, after all. She shrugged it off.

"Mmm, this pizza smells good," she told him. Maybe she could eat at least one piece.

"It tastes even better," he said with a smile that showed his dimples. "Dig in."

The night air felt colder to Amber when they walked out of the warm restaurant to Mick's truck, and she shivered.

"Cold?" Mick asked as he unlocked the passenger door.

"A little," she admitted.

"I'll get the truck warmed up pretty quick. Up you go," he said as he boosted her up into the truck. Again, she could have done it herself, but she liked the feel of his strong arms. It had been a long time since she'd gone out with a man—in fact, she couldn't even remember when. She'd worked long hours and weekends at the law firm. There wasn't any time to meet a man, much less date.

Once they were on the road again, Mick said, "You should come out and see my horses sometime.

Have you ever ridden a horse?" He looked at her.

"I rode a pony once at someone's birthday party. The guy led him around. Does that count?"

"Well, not really. Would you like to ride a horse?"

"I think they're really beautiful, majestic animals, and I've enjoyed getting to know Sugar and Spice," she hedged.

"Yeah, they're good horses, but then they're pretty much retired, like most of Bob and Nancy's animals."

"Why do they have all those animals anyway?"

"Most—or maybe all of them—are rescues." Amber must have looked as puzzled as she felt, because Mick explained. "You know—animals nobody else wants. For instance, Samantha chases birds, and one night they came home and found she'd cornered a rooster. She'd injured him a bit, so Bob put him in a box and kept him there until he healed. And then Nancy put some signs up, and called around, but no one claimed him. So Bob made the coop, and Nancy named him Jake. And then, Nancy said she thought he might be lonely, so they got Jackie at the feed store.

"I think when they got Sugar, Nancy planned to do some jumping—you've probably seen those old jumps set up in the pasture." When Amber shook her head, he continued. "But then she found out how old Sugar really is—twenty-five—so she's just a pasture pet. Then I guess they thought Sugar might be lonely, so they looked for a companion for her.

Somebody at the feed store knew about Spice, so they got him. Bob thought he might take up reining like some of their friends do, but then he found out Spice has arthritis in his front legs—he'd been used pretty hard on that dude ranch where he came from—so, he's just a pasture ornament too like the rest of 'em. Bob and Nancy can afford it. They have good jobs. Nancy refers to the animals as their 'kids.'"

"What about the cows, chickens, goats and Woolie, the sheep? Are they all rescues too?"

"Yup." He looked over at her again. "You never really answered my question."

"I know." She sighed. "My brother's fiancée wants to take me riding sometime. She keeps her horse at her uncle's farm in Cle Elum. But when I worked at the law firm, it was hard for me to take the time off and go with her. And now…well, last year she took my brother Blake riding and he got hurt—pretty bad…" she trailed off.

"So you're afraid you might get hurt?" he guessed.

"Yeah, I guess that's it." She sighed.

"Maybe you just need the right teacher." He smiled. "I do a little training and riding instruction on the side when I have time. Usually, people bring their horses to me, but if you want, you could ride Buck. He's pretty gentle." When she didn't respond, he looked at her again. "Will you think about it?"

"I will." Another silence. "What was that Sue saying about Buck and her new colt? Something about a tiger?"

Mick laughed. "Kiger. Kiger Mustang. They come from the Steens Mountain area in southeastern Oregon. Most wild horses are mixed breeds, but Kiger Mustangs have many characteristics of the original Spanish Mustang. Spanish Mustangs were a part of early American history, with roots in Native American history, and are the horses that helped settle the west. At one time, they were thought to be extinct. Since the Kiger Mustangs may be one of the best remaining examples of the Spanish Mustang, their preservation is really important. Kigers are usually a buckskin color. That's why I named mine 'Buck,'" he explained. He looked at her and laughed again. "Too much information, huh? Well, you asked." He shrugged.

When they got back to the house, and pulled up to the gate, before Mick could get out, Amber put a hand on his arm to stop him. "I can get it, Mick. My knee's much better. In fact, it doesn't even hurt, so if you need to get home, you can let me off here and I'll walk back to the house."

He shrugged again. "If that's what you want." Amber felt a bit surprised and maybe a little disappointed when he agreed so readily. But when she didn't leap at the chance to take riding lessons from him, maybe he'd given up on her and decided to stick with women like Mardie, Sue and Diane who obviously shared his enthusiasm for horses—and probably for him too. She'd seen the way they eyed him. She could imagine that many women were mesmerized by the rugged shoer's muscled arms and bright blue eyes. But despite his good looks, he didn't seem to be full of himself.

Amber slid down from the truck's high seat, turned around to shut the door, and was surprised to see Mick not in the driver's seat. She turned back to face the gate and saw him unlocking it. When he held it open to let her through, he said, "I'll walk you to the house. My mama would have a fit if I left you here." He waved an arm. "After you."

As the snow crunched under their boots, Amber thought, if not for the snow, the night would be pitch-black. She looked up at the sky and gasped in awe.

"What's the matter?" Mick asked her in a concerned voice.

"There must be a million stars up there, strewn across the sky." She pointed. "I've never seen anything like it except in pictures. It's beautiful."

"That's because it's so dark out here in the country with no streetlights."

"I see the Big Dipper…and the Little Dipper." She breathed in the icy air.

Mick stood closer to her and pointed. "And there's Orion. See it?"

"No. Where?" She shivered as she stood there trying to find it, then felt the warmth of Mick's heavily-muscled arm around her, as he pointed with his other hand.

"Right there. If you could wish on a star right now. What would you wish?"

"I'd wish that this night hadn't been a dream."

He took her arm and slowly turned her to face him. He touched her cheek. She never in her life had a man look at her the way Mick was now. Their breath mingled in the icy air. His handsome face was lit by the moonlight.

He dropped his head to kiss her. It began with just a brush of his lips to hers. When she wound her hands behind his neck, he deepened the kiss. With his arms around her, he held her as though she was special. Precious.

When he finally stepped back, he said, "You must be cold. You'd better get inside. Come on, I'll walk you to the door."

Amber felt acutely aware of his solid male body next to hers. She was glad for the warmth of his arm. He kept it around her as they continued to the house. Was he just being thoughtful, trying to keep her warm? If not, what might happen when they reached the door? She shivered again with anticipation—not from cold this time, but Mick wouldn't know that, and held her a little tighter.

When they reached the house, Mick wordlessly slipped his arm off her shoulders, and she missed the warmth. But then he held out his hand and helped her up the wide steps, and across the deck, slippery with melting, slushy snow. When she put the key in the front door's lock, she heard the dogs bark. "Maybe you'd better stand back before I open this door. The dogs will probably come barreling out," Amber warned him with a laugh.

"I should go. I need to do some studying yet tonight," Mick replied as he stepped aside and they watched the dogs frolic in the snow after they took care of business.

"Oh, okay." Amber felt a little let down, but also apprehensive, and her knees felt weak. Would he kiss her again?

His eyes stared straight into hers for moment, and then he took a step toward her. As if in slow motion, she watched one arm pull her to him. Then he lowered his head several inches to hers and brushed a kiss across her lips.

She resisted the urge to close her eyes and lean her head on his shoulder.

But he stepped back again. "I had a good time tonight, Amber," he said softly. "I hope you did too."

She nodded.

"Good." He paused. "Well, let me know if you're interested in riding sometime, okay?" He gave her shoulder a one-armed squeeze, then turned and walked down the steps. At the bottom, he turned and looked back at her. "Good night," he said, and then headed for his truck.

"Good night. Be careful out there," she called after him. As she watched him walk, she called out to the dogs to come back. They did and she opened the door to let them back in the house, and then turned to look out at the road, just in time to see Mick climb into his truck. He honked the horn and she waved and then walked into the house, shutting the door behind her.

****

As Mick drove away from Bob and Nancy's

place, he thought back over the evening with Amber. Man, her lips felt amazing and kissing her made him wish he could have more. But, he reminded himself again, he didn't have time for this. If he didn't put the brakes on now, one thing would surely lead to another…He shook his head. No, he'd better just stop it now.

He just hoped she didn't think the kisses meant more than they did.

Chapter Eight

Amber wanted to talk to another woman. She would have called a girlfriend, but on a Saturday night, she figured everyone would be out. Besides, she didn't want to have to answer a bunch of questions. She picked up her cell phone and punched in Brenda's number.

"Amber?" Brenda said. "Are you okay? Is anything wrong?" Her brother's fiancée sounded concerned.

"Everything's fine. In fact, it's warming up and if it melts enough, I think I'll drive back to the apartment tomorrow and check my mailbox."

"We're moving you out next weekend, right?"

"Yup, that's the plan, as long as you all are still available to do it."

"Do you want to talk to Blake?"

"No, not this time. Actually, I called to talk to you."

"Sure. What's up? Do you need to know something about horses?"

"No, it's...well, it's kind of a man problem."

"You're asking me?" Brenda sounded surprised and Amber figured she had a right to be, considering their history. They hadn't always gotten along.

"Yeah, you've put up with my brother off and on all these years. And, well, you probably dated when you two were apart..." she trailed off, not sure if it was a sore subject, but heck, they were back together, and this time for good."

"Uh-huh," Brenda said in such a way that gave Amber a clue she wasn't alone.

"Blake's right there, isn't he?"

"Yes, but go ahead. We have nothing to hide from each other." She laughed and Amber heard a muffled voice.

"Well, I've kinda met this guy..."

"Really?"

She sounds way too excited, Amber thought.

"It's really no big deal," she said hastily. "In fact, I probably won't see him again. He lives way up here and I'll be going back to Seattle." Brenda didn't say anything, didn't interrupt or ask any questions, so Amber felt encouraged to continue, and gave the other woman a brief version of her time spent with Mick.

"Well, of course I don't know the man, but it seems to me he's put the ball in your court. He's certainly shown his interest in you—bringing the books, helping you with the animals, taking you to town and dinner, and inviting you to ride his horse—even an offer for riding lessons."

"I suppose, but I'm not like those women he talked to at the restaurant. I don't ride. I don't know anything about farming and animals. I'm a city girl."

"Sounds to me like you're making excuses."

"Excuses?"

"Reasons why he wouldn't like you. Take him up on his offer for a riding lesson," Brenda urged.

"What if I get hurt?"

"You're thinking of your brother, aren't you…or do you mean…"

"I don't know, Brenda. Maybe both."

"Sometimes you just have to take chances, Amber," Brenda said softly, maybe thinking of herself.

Amber went silent for a moment. "Yeah, maybe you're right. Will you and Blake be home tomorrow, or do you have to work?" They talked a few minutes more and then hung up. Brenda certainly gave her a lot to think about.

Amber heard the patter of rain on the skylights in the living room when she sat in a recliner with her laptop computer—and laptop cats. One sat on each armrest. *Good,* she thought. *Hopefully it will melt the rest of the snow and the roads will be clear enough for a non-snow driver like me to venture out.*

But when she let the dogs out the next morning, there was still a lot of slush on the driveway. She stood on the porch to get a better view of the road, and saw the dogs trotting up to the gate. What was Samantha doing? And then she realized that the slush along the driveway was actually water and the Husky was wading in it and drinking it. "Saa-maaan-thaa!" she called, but the dog ignored her. Shoot. She'd have to get dressed and bring her in. It was too cold for the dog to be out wading in cold water. She needed to find some old towels and dry Samantha off.

The rest of the morning didn't go any better. When Amber looked into the stalls as she did the morning feeding, she saw that they were full of mud and ice. What was it Mick said the other day about stall cleaning? She'd ask Mandy. And she needed to call her family and tell them she couldn't come for a visit today after all. She could only hope that tomorrow the roads were clear.

When Amber called the neighbors and asked Mandy about stall cleaning, she said, "Oh yeah, I guess I forgot to tell you about that too. I just do that kind of thing automatically. Maybe I'd better come over there and show you where things are and stuff."

Amber again asked if she needed a ride, crossing her fingers and hoping the teen would say she didn't. She breathed a sigh of relief when the girl said her brother could drop her off. She set her phone down and put her coat, boots and gloves back on. Amber had the key now that Mandy used, so she needed to unlock the gate. Samantha whined when she walked to the door.

"Sorry, pup. You need to stay in here and dry off." She hadn't been able to find any ratty old towels, so she'd used her hair dryer instead to get the Husky as dry as possible. Now she just needed to dry out the rest of the way in the warm house. The smell of wet dog permeated the air and Amber felt almost glad she needed to go out again. Phew. "You stay here too, Bruiser," she said when both dogs blocked her escape. "I'll be back soon." It was a lie, but she doubted they could tell time.

An unfamiliar pickup truck pulled into the space in front of the gate. Amber's heartbeat quickened. Could it be Mick? Maybe he had more than one truck. She hurried as fast as possible in the slush, across the yard and driveway to the gate. But her hopes fell when Mandy slid off the seat and out of the cab. Amber didn't want to make her wait and tried to hurry, but when she reached for the lock, and then tried to insert the key, it wouldn't go in.

"It's frozen," Mandy said and turned to the driver of the truck. "Josh, give me your lighter." She reached into the truck and came back out with a lighter in one hand, and her crutches in the other. Walking slowly forward, she leaned on the crutches when she reached the gate, picked up the padlock and flicked the lighter with her other hand. After a couple of tries, the key slid in and turned. The lock popped open.

"Hey, that's a great trick," Amber said with a smile. "I don't smoke, but I can see that a lighter might be a handy thing to have around."

Mandy tossed it to her. "Here, keep it. Josh has plenty, right bro?" Mandy called to her brother. Before he had time to protest, she slammed the passenger side door of the old truck and waved him off. "Okay, let's go. My mom is coming to get me in a few," she said to Amber and headed toward the barn. "Hey, was Mick here last night? Josh brought me back from my 4-H meeting and I saw his truck in the driveway. Are the horses all right?" the teenager asked as Amber used the pitchfork.

Amber blushed, and hesitated before she answered, not quite sure what to say. "Yeah, they're fine."

"So, why—"the girl started to ask a question, but Amber found a way to divert her attention.

"Am I doing this right?"

"Yes, but—" This time she stopped at the sound of a car honk out at the road. "Oh, that must be my mom. Gotta go," Mandy told Amber—all too soon, or just in time for her to avoid more of the girl's questions—and left her to the cleaning.

Amber walked to the first stall pushing a wheelbarrow with a shovel and pitchfork clattering around in it. She followed Mandy's instructions and gagged at the smell. She'd hoped the stall's occupants would be outside, but they didn't all cooperate. Sugar appeared to be very curious about what she was doing—or maybe just hoping for more food. Amber twice persuaded her with a push to leave. And then she just stood there, slowly turned her head around and looked at Amber as though she couldn't believe Amber would do such a thing.

"Sorry, girl, but you'll be glad when it's clean again." Amber tried to placate the mare. Sugar finally gave up trying to get back in her stall when Amber blocked the door with the wheelbarrow.

Heidi did the same thing. When Amber entered the front of the stall, the Brown Swiss shoved her with her big brown cow head. Amber petted her face and Heidi let out a low moo and leaned harder into Amber's hand, so she scrubbed the cow's face with her fingers. Amber laughed.

"If you were a cat, you'd purr, wouldn't you girl?"

The worst part of the whole dirty job was trying to push the wheelbarrow through the slush and mud when she got to the compost pile behind the barn. The wheelbarrow kept getting stuck in the mud, and one time she got stuck for a moment and walked out of her rubber boot. She grabbed the wheelbarrow and hopped back on one foot to retrieve her boot, desperately hoping she wouldn't fall.

"Yuck," said when she reached for the stuck boot and found some of the muck inside. Gingerly, she eased her foot back inside it. "Ugh."

Amber never felt so happy to finish a job. She headed for the shower as soon as she got back in the house. She'd left her boots outside, even though she'd walked through Samantha's "wading pool" out front to clean them off.

That night, she felt stiff and sore, having used muscles she didn't normally use on her rather sedentary job. She'd heard that farmers went to bed early and now she understood why. She felt to tired from the physical labor and the early feedings, and again found herself nodding off early that night. Oh well, she thought as she brushed her teeth. With all the rain falling now, the slush would be gone by morning and she could get an early start on her drive to Seattle. Normally a person who had a hard time getting to sleep, she had no problem that night.

Amber rushed through her chores that morning, happy to see that the previous night's rain did the trick and melted the snow. Blake and Brenda would probably be at work and her parent's too, but maybe she could meet a friend for lunch and do a little shopping after she picked up her mail at the apartment. She gave the animals a little extra feed and pets to make up for leaving them, and left the farm at eight-thirty. By then, she hoped the morning commute should be over. She turned the volume way up on her car radio and sang along to her favorite tunes. It felt good to get out again. The country was okay, but she was a city girl.

Amber had driven half-way down the hill on the winding road that led to the valley, when she saw something white in the middle of the road. She slowed down when she realized it was a sign: Water Over Roadway, Road Closed Ahead.

What? Amber inched the car forward and stopped abruptly when she saw the horrifying scene below. "Oh gee, the whole town's underwater."

Amber sat there for a moment, thinking. Now what? She didn't know any other way to get to the freeway. "Oh wait, I bet I can go through Stanwood." There wasn't enough room to turn around, so she backed the car up the hill, hoping all the while that no one else would try to drive down. Thankfully, she got the car turned around in a dairy farm's driveway, and headed back the way she'd come, and past the mini farm on the road to Stanwood. But when she came to the **T** in the road, she saw the same sign. With a sigh, she backed up again, turned around in another driveway and headed back to the house. Then she remembered Mick saying it usually flooded a couple of times a year around there.

Stuck inside again, Amber decided it was a good time to look for a job. She sat down at the dining room table and opened up her laptop. She remembered something else Mick said: "They have lawyers in this town, you know."

Just for the heck of it, she looked at legal jobs in Snohomish County—silly of course, but just for fun. There were a couple in Everett at the courthouse…and then she saw it. She read the job description…"Small, friendly office in downtown Stanwood needs a paralegal/office manager for two attorneys. Bonuses." Intrigued, she picked up the phone and dialed the number, but it just rang and rang, until finally a recorded voice came on. Amber smacked her head with her hand. Of course. No one could get to Stanwood because of the flooding. She powered her cell phone off and searched the Internet again.

She gasped as she found an overhead shot that showed a farm on the back road to Stanwood. It was surrounded by water. The article from the newspaper said that a half mile of formerly dry fields was covered with water in five minutes. When the Stillaguamish River overflowed it cut the small town below her off from the rest of the county. The town's water system quit working and firefighters filled up a makeshift pool so the people living there would have water to drink.

And in Stanwood, workers used a backhoe to build a four-foot concrete-block wall across the main highway. No wonder she couldn't go in either direction.

Would she *ever* get back to Seattle?

Chapter Nine

The waters finally receded by Wednesday morning and Amber was able to follow a detour route that took her out to the freeway.

She felt surprised to find the freeway still so crowded—rush hour should have ended. It took her far longer than she'd planned to reach Seattle.

She drove to her apartment first, and though she usually parked on the street, this time there weren't any spaces available in front of her building. She circled the block a couple times hoping someone would pull out, but with no success, so she finally settled on a spot a block away.

When she unlocked her apartment door, it smelled musty inside and she shivered at the cold. She turned the thermostat up a little, but didn't want to add to her heating bill, so turned it back off as soon as it warmed up a little. She opened a window to air out the place and heard the constant noise of the traffic on her busy street. When she walked outside to empty her garbage into the dumpster, she smelled the exhaust of the city bus. Why hadn't she ever noticed the noise and smells before? And when she walked back into her apartment, it felt cold and unwelcoming with no animals there to talk to or greet her at the door.

The phone rang and when Amber picked it

up, she saw it was her mother. "Hi Mom."

"Hi, dear. Did you make it into town?"

"Yeah, I'm here at the apartment. What time is it?"

"One-thirty. I called to see if you want to come over for dinner."

Amber sighed. She missed her mom's cooking. "I wish I could, Mom, but I still have to go to the post office and I need to finish packing so everything will be ready to move this weekend. And then, the traffic is so bad I'll have to go right back north. I have to feed the animals."

"Well, you've certainly become quite the farmer," her mother remarked with a laugh. "But I'm glad you take your job so seriously."

"Thanks, Mom."

"Well okay, dear. I have to get back to work. I'm sorry we won't see you tonight, but we'll see you this weekend for sure, right?"

"Yes Mom. I'll be here, come Hell or high water—oh, I'd better not say that. Who knows? There could be another flood," Amber said and sighed.

The commute took forever—or so it seemed to Amber—back north from Seattle. She'd gotten a later start back than she'd hoped. Unfortunately, her final check from the law firm wasn't waiting in her mailbox. It didn't help her mood as she sat in bumper-to-bumper traffic in Everett, worse than the time she and Brenda drove up to check out her job there. She'd never driven in such a mess and realized what she had missed taking a bus to work. There was no way she could handle this twice a day, five days a week. But of course, she wouldn't have to. Soon, she would be back in Seattle—or somewhere. That was still the big question. She hadn't heard from any of her friends since she'd taken this job, and still couldn't believe Justine hadn't texted her back about lunch. Where would she stay? And with no job, she couldn't get another apartment yet. Maybe she'd have to sleep on her parents' couch in the family room after all, with her nephews' toys spread out around her.

Samantha and Bruiser raced to the gate to greet her. Bruiser of course, rushed furiously up to the gate, barked and showed his teeth. But when she got out of the car, he gave her a couple more half-hearted woofs, then grinned and waved his tail.

"Bruiser, you old faker," she told him, but she didn't reach over the gate to pet him—she knew better. "Hi Sammy," she said to the Husky, reached out to pet her, and got a big slurpy kiss. "Thanks, girl."

As she walked from the car to the house, Amber was greeted by a neigh, followed by a moo or two, a baa from Woolie, and then a whole chorus of sounds. Music to her ears. She'd never felt so welcome and glad to be home. Home? When did this become home? Oddly, it felt more like home than her apartment now.

Thursday, Amber renewed her search for a job. She sent cover letters and resumes to several possibilities and finally got a phone interview scheduled for two o'clock that afternoon. Her stomach growled and she looked up at the kitchen clock. One o'clock. She'd missed lunch again, she'd been so absorbed in her job search. She'd better eat something so her stomach didn't growl during the interview.

Amber glanced out the tall windows and saw sunshine. She stood up from the table, stretched and walked over to the windows. When she looked out to the pasture she saw Spice standing guard over Sugar and the cows lying down nearby, soaking up the sun. She looked in the other direction and saw the dogs stretched out on the grass, sunning themselves too. Why was she inside the house on such a glorious day? She grabbed a yogurt from the refrigerator and walked out to the deck, where she sank into a bright green Adirondack chair. The winter air was a little nippy in the shade, but there in the sun, it felt heavenly. Amber tilted her face up to the sky and closed her eyes.

A sudden commotion caught her attention. She opened her eyes and looked toward the sound which seemed to come from the pasture. Sugar stood up. Amber watched as the horse took a few steps. Something wasn't right.

Amber rose from the chair, walked down the steps and over to the pasture fence.

"Come here, Sugar," she called to the mare, hoping she would obey without a bribe. Amber held out her hand, but the horse just stood there. "Hold on. I'll be right back." Amber ran back to the house and grabbed the piece of bread she'd gotten out to make a sandwich. Sugar loved bread.

This time, Sugar raised her head and took a few hesitant steps, but Amber could tell how much it hurt her. Oh crap. What should she do? Amber threw the bread and luckily it landed within a few inches of the horse's nose. Then she turned around and ran back to the house again. Mandy was in school. Maybe her mother or someone else was home. They owned horses; they should know what to do. But the phone just rang and rang. She looked at the clock. Brenda was still at work, but maybe she would answer. She punched in the number.

As soon as Brenda answered, Amber exclaimed, "Sugar is hurt and I don't know what to do!"

"Wh-what? Amber, is this you?"

"Yes! Sugar—you know, one of the horses—can hardly walk!" she exclaimed in a panic into the phone.

"What happened?"

"I don't know. I wasn't there. I mean, I was there, but I didn't see what happened."

"Did you look at her…you know, up close?" Brenda asked.

"No, it wouldn't do any good. I still wouldn't know what to do."

"Where's Mandy?"

"She's at school and no one answers at her parents' house. What would you do?"

"Hmm. Well, if it was Carrot and I wasn't available I'd want you to call the shoer. Call—what's his name—Mick?"

"Thanks Brenda." Amber ended the call without another word and called Mick. As she waited for the phone to connect, she heard the phone beep. She looked up to the wall clock again and saw that it was two o'clock. Oh no, the phone interview. Just then the call connected.

"Mick Christopher...Amber, is this you?"

"Yes!" Amber nearly shouted. "She can't walk!"

After she explained the situation and ended the call, she realized she hadn't asked when he'd be there. He might have been in the midst of shoeing or driving to his next appointment. When the phone rang, she thought it might be him calling her back.

"Yes?" she answered, a little out of breath after arguing with Bruiser about coming in.

"Is this Amber Preston?" a woman asked.

"Yes."

"This is Sally Goodwin from Templeton and Howe. I scheduled a phone interview for you at two this afternoon..."

"Oh yes," Amber said. "I'm so sorry. I have an emergency at home." The other woman didn't reply immediately and Amber figured she'd heard it all; all the excuses for missing an interview.

"Well, I'll see if we can reschedule—if you're still interested," the woman said in a frosty tone, Amber thought.

"Yes, I'd like that," she replied, but a flash of

light caught her eye and she looked out the window to see Mick's pickup truck at the gate. "I'm sorry, I have to go. Can I call you back and reschedule?" she said hastily into the phone.

"Very well," the woman replied and hung up.

Amber doubted she would get another chance when she called back, but what could she do? Sugar was important.

She felt relieved when Mick walked through the gate.

She'd brought another piece of bread for Sugar in case they had trouble catching her, but it wasn't necessary; the mare hadn't moved. Mick handed her the horse's rope and stroked the mare's nose, then knelt down and examined her. He carefully ran his hand up and down Sugar's legs. Finally, he beckoned for her to crouch down next to him.

"I think I've found the problem."

"Do you think Spice kicked her?"

"No. It looks more like a puncture wound in her hoof from something she stepped on," he told her. I'll clean it out and give her some Bute.

"What's 'Butte'? Isn't that a town in Montana?"

"Phenylbutazone or b-u-t-e is a pain medicine. I'll give you the pills I keep on hand. You have to crush them up and then put them in her grain with some molasses to make the powder stick. She should like that, she has a sweet tooth." He smiled. Then we'll wrap her foot and you'll need to soak it every day—" He must have heard her gasp when he said, "You'll need to soak it," as he stopped talking and looked at her for a moment then nodded. "Okay, let's get her in her stall and then I'll show you what to do."

Amber watched him carefully, glad that Sugar seemed content to just stand there in her stall while Mick worked on her hoof. Amber nodded when he showed her each step of the process, but she wished she could write it down.

When he finished, he pulled a red bandanna out of his back pocket and wiped his hands. "I need to get to my next appointment. Do you think you can handle this tomorrow morning?"

"I'll have to, won't I?" But she didn't know how.

"Call if you need me. I'll keep my phone on." He gathered up the items he'd brought from the truck. "Walk with me to the gate?"

"Sure." She followed him and watched as he reached through the open canopy on the back of his truck and dropped the items into a wooden caddy. Then he turned to her and resting both arms over her shoulders, gave her a hug. "Don't worry. She'll be fine...and so will you," he said, gave her a quick kiss and swung up into his truck.

Before she turned back to the house, Amber looked up, and saw Mick wave at her as he drove off. She lifted her hand and waved back but her mind was on the added chore and poor Sugar—and his kiss.

Chapter Ten

Amber hurried back into the house and called the law firm back, in hopes she could salvage the interview. "Sally Goodwin, please," she said when the receptionist answered.

"Who shall I say is calling?"

"Amber Preston. I need to reschedule my interview."

There was a short pause, and then, "I'll connect you."

But the phone just rang and rang and finally went to voicemail. Amber left an apologetic message and told Sally how much she looked forward to the interview. She hung up with a sigh, and very much doubted she'd get a call back.

Now that she was no longer concentrating on the phone, she heard a loud banging noise outside.

"What is that?" she asked the cats who snoozed on the floor and a chair. She rose from her seat at the dining room table and walked to the windows. She couldn't see anything obvious. "I'd better go and check it out," she told them. She grabbed her coat from the peg on the wall in the entryway and sat down on the bench there to pull on her boots.

Outside, Bruiser sniffed and yipped at the barn door. "What is it, guy?" she asked him. She began to feel a little afraid. What if someone was in there?

When she slowly slid the door open, Sugar let out a loud neigh. She tossed her head up and down. Amber saw Spice standing several yards away out in the pasture, calmly grazing on what little grass was still there.

"What's the matter, girl?" She walked over to the stall where Sugar had thrown her hay all over, including into her water bucket. She'd eaten the grain with the crushed pills mixed with molasses Amber gave her when Mick put her in the stall, but Amber didn't want to give her any more. Mandy seemed very adamant that Sugar could easily overeat and couldn't have much grain.

"Are you bored? Or do you just want a treat? I'll get some more bread. Be back in a sec," Amber told the horse. She ran out of the barn and back to the house, Bruiser and Samantha running ahead in excitement.

But after Sugar gobbled the bread, she turned and limped over to the back of her stall, and gazed longingly outside, pushing against the mesh nylon gate that kept her in. "You don't like it in here, do you? You want to be outside, huh?" Amber felt bad for the horse. She probably felt as though she was in jail. Should she put Spice inside to keep Sugar company? But Spice didn't need to be inside and then he'd be unhappy too. She needed to do something. Sugar was so agitated, pacing around the stall, Amber was afraid she'd tear the bandages off her hoof. Maybe she should call Mick. He must have experience with this kind of thing. He'd told her to call anytime.

She pulled the number up on her smart phone and called.

"Hello, Amber?" Mick answered after the first ring. After she'd explained the problem he said, "Hmm…I haven't had much experience with this, but I know that Thoroughbred farms use goats to keep the horses company. Maybe you could try it."

"Well… okay. Thanks Mick. I'd better let you go." She was about to hang up when he spoke again.

"Amber, I've been thinking…"

"Yes?"

"You seemed a little uncertain about changing Sugar's dressing. Would you like me to help you with it the first time?"

"That would be great. That would really take a weight off my mind," she babbled in delight. She'd been worried about it most of the day since he left. But then another thought crossed her mind. "But I don't want to make you late for your appointments," she said reluctantly.

"No worries. I'll stop by early in the morning. Does seven o'clock work for you?"

"Sure. Thanks Mick." She walked off in search of the goats.

Amber had just finished dinner when her cell phone rang. She looked at the number.

"Hi Mick."

"Hi yourself. I just called to see how Sugar's doing. Did you put the goats in with her?"

"When I let them in the barn, she seemed interested. I was kind of afraid to put them in the stall with her. They're so small and she was so agitated, I left them in the barn to wander around. It seemed to calm her down." She didn't tell him about the mess she'd found when she went back to feed. The goats got into everything and left little gifts behind as well. "And then after I fed awhile ago, I left Spice in his stall for the night."

"Great. Sounds like that took care of it, then."

"Yeah, that was a good idea. Thanks again."

"See you in the morning."

For some reason, Amber couldn't get to sleep that night. She listened to the ticking of the grandfather clock and found herself counting the deep dongs that it made on the hour and half hour. The first couple of nights she'd stayed there, she'd found it hard to sleep because of the clock, but after that she didn't notice it anymore—until tonight.

Or maybe she couldn't sleep because the frog chorus sounded particularly loud. The first night she heard them, she didn't know where the noise came from. But one day, she found Samantha about to pounce on something. At first, she didn't see anything in the ornamental rock and beauty bark of the dry flower bed, but then she realized the large piece of bark was a tiny frog. "Samantha! Shoo! Leave that poor little frog alone!" she shouted at the dog. When the Husky ran off after Bruiser, Amber looked at the frog more closely. Should she pick it up and move it somewhere safe? She looked around. She didn't trust Samantha not to come back when she left. She'd seen Samantha watching the birds in a bush, just waiting for one to get close enough. When Amber looked back down, the little frog wasn't there. But suddenly, she heard a loud *ribbit*. She couldn't believe the tiny thing made such a loud sound.

The only other reason she couldn't sleep could be that she'd set the alarm to make sure she got up early enough to be dressed and ready when Mick came to help her with Sugar. She'd gotten so used to getting up to feed the animals she no longer needed to set the alarm for that. For some reason she didn't understand, when she set the alarm for a different time, it made it hard for her to sleep…

Oh heck, admit it. You can't sleep because you know you're going to see him in the morning.

Amber tossed and turned so many times both cats gave up and jumped off the bed.

When she woke the next morning, Amber felt as though she'd just gone to sleep. She wanted to stay in the nice warm bed, but she remembered with a start that she needed to get up early. She didn't remember the alarm going off. She looked at the clock. Oh no. Either it went off and she didn't hear it, or she didn't set the alarm right. Mick would be there in ten minutes.

Amber hastily dressed and followed the dogs out the door. As soon as her feet hit the ground, she ran across the yard and driveway to the front gate, the dogs racing ahead of her. Of course, they reached it first and turned around to gloat, it seemed. She could swear Samantha smiled at her, and Bruiser woofed.

"Okay, okay, you beat me. Proud of yourselves, are you? Let me remind you, you have four legs and I—" She stopped and looked up when she heard Mick's truck at the gate. The door opened and he stepped out.

"Good morning."

Did he see her talking to the dogs? Embarrassed, Amber felt her cheeks burn. "Hi."

"Are you ready?'

"That's Spice," she explained at the sound of a hoof hitting a wall and loud nickering. "He always lets me know when he's ready to eat."

"Well, we'll try to be quick then so he can eat—unless you want to feed him first. But I imagine that will upset Sugar," he added. He turned to her and she saw the smile on his face. In fact, now that she thought about it, he smiled most of the time.

"I think you're right, though I wish I could feed everyone first. But you need to get to work and I don't want to take up more of your time. I really appreciate you coming out this morning."

"Glad I could help. I had a feeling it wasn't something you felt comfortable with yet." He grinned.

"You're right." Amber slid the barn door open and they walked inside. "Excuse me a sec." She walked over to the grain container and with the large scooper, dumped some oats into a small bucket. She gave all the animals in their stalls a small amount of grain to appease them, then put the bucket down and opened the door to Sugar's stall, pulled the halter and rope from the hook, and walked up to the mare. As Sugar crunched on the grain, Amber pulled the halter over her nose and up and around her ears, then fastened it and grabbed the lead rope.

"Ready now?" Mick asked her.

"Yeah." She sighed.

He knelt down in the fragrant shavings and unhooked the clips that kept the Ace bandages on tight, and then pulled the sticky, colorful wrap off. As he continued to strip off the dressing, Amber caught a whiff of his cologne—or maybe aftershave. Whatever, it smelled good. She knew she should pay attention to what he was doing, but she couldn't help studying him—fresh shaven cheeks, thick black hair, crisp blue cotton shirt, tight-fitting worn blue jeans, and brown work boots.

"Okay, now you'll want to clean this off and...do you have a bucket and some warm or hot water?" His voice broke into her thoughts.

"Oh, that's right, you said I needed to soak her hoof. Um, I need to get some water in the house...Can you hold her or should I tie her up?" *Pay attention*, she told herself.

"I'll take the rope," he reached up and gently pulled it from her grasp, and as he did their eyes met. Amber felt so mesmerized by his piercing blue eyes, it took her a moment to realize she hadn't moved or fully let go of the rope. Mick leaned in and kissed her.

"Uh…uh, I'll be right back." She hastily dropped the end of the rope, turned, stepped out of the stall and scurried across the concrete barn floor to the door. She felt sure her face must be a bright red. She could feel the slow burn spread across her cheeks and welcomed the cold air when she hurried through the door and outside. When Amber walked back to the barn with the bucket of hot water, she told herself, "Ignore the man and pay attention to what you need to learn." After all, he wouldn't be there tomorrow morning and she'd be on her own.

But there he stood in the stall, holding the rope, feeding Sugar some kind of treats from his pockets, and talking in a soft, soothing voice to the horse.

"Now Sugar, we're just trying to help you. You need to be good to Amber. She's new at this. You don't want her to get a bad impression of horses—particularly you—now do you?"

And then he must have heard her approach. He looked up and smiled at her, as though happy to see her. She shook her head to clear it of those thoughts. Concentrate. "Okay, here's the water," she said cheerfully. "What's next?"

"First, we get her hoof into the bucket. Do you have the Epsom Salts?" She handed them to him. "We'll soak her hoof for awhile and then put on more medicine and clean bandages. And…you'll need to keep the stall clean as well.

"Oh. Right."

Fortunately—or maybe because of the talk Mick had with her—Sugar cooperated and picked up her hoof for him, then let him put it back down in the black rubber bucket. To make sure she kept it there, he told Amber, he held onto her lower leg. Then they waited. Amber couldn't help looking up at the apple-shaped clock on the barn wall. It seemed as though all of this took a long time. Didn't he need to get to work? He must have noticed her glance at the clock. "Don't worry, I still have a few minutes till I have to leave."

After a bit, Mick looked at his watch. "Okay, if you'll hand me that towel, I'll dry off her hoof and you can apply the medicine and then wrap it. Thanks," he said as she handed him the towel.

What? Amber felt panicky. She thought he would do the rest of it. She wasn't ready. "Oh, couldn't you do it today and then I'll do it tomorrow? I think I need to watch you one more time."

He looked up at her. "I could, but don't you think you'll remember better if you do some of the work yourself with me here to observe?"

He had a great smile. It was mesmerizing. She found herself wanting to do anything he asked.

"Well, I suppose I should..."

When they'd finished Amber felt good about herself. She could do it, no problem—easy. Mick even clapped her on the shoulder. "Think you've got it?"

"Oh yeah, no problem."

"Okay then, I have to run." He pulled his coat

on that he'd hung over the stall door, and Amber walked outside with him.

"Thanks again, Mick. I couldn't have done it without you." This time she beamed.

"You're welcome. But if you have any problems, don't hesitate to call. I'd be happy to come out again tomorrow."

"Don't worry, I can do it now," she answered. Well that was stupid. It would be a great excuse to see him again. She thought he looked a little disappointed. "But I'll call if I do need help," she hastily added.

Chapter Eleven

Amber called her parents' house Friday night to see if her brothers and dad still planned to move her out of the apartment the next day. She talked to her dad and he assured her they would meet her at the apartment complex at noon. She figured that gave her plenty of time to get the animals fed and Sugar's dressing changed.

Saturday morning, Amber got up a little earlier than usual. She woke and thought about all the things she needed to do before she drove to Seattle. Finally, wide awake, and no longer able to sleep, she got out of bed. She dressed in her outdoor clothes, then pulled on her boots and headed out the door with the dogs as they led the way to the barn.

This time, Spice nickered and tossed his head up and down, not happy it seemed, about staying in all night with Sugar.

"Okay, okay, you'll be first," she assured him, and hurried to the feed room to get the grain. As promised, she fed Spice his grain first, but then gave Sugar her grain and hay so she would be finished by the time Amber came back to work with her.

After she'd fed all the outdoor animals, walked back inside the house, fed the cats and dogs, and filled the small bucket with hot water, she carried it out to the barn and up to Sugar's stall.

"Ready girl?" she asked the horse as she petted her neck. "I sure hope so." Her guts twisted with nerves, and her hands felt wet inside her gloves. She pulled them off, and wiped her hands across her jeans. "This is stupid. Why am I so nervous?" she asked herself. "Let's get started before the water turns cold," she said as she walked into the stall.

Twenty minutes later, Amber rued the day she'd agreed to take the job. She was not a horseperson. It seemed that everything that could go wrong, did, probably starting with her interpretation of Sugar's first head toss. The mare seemed to have woken up on the wrong side of the stall. She wouldn't stand still, so Amber put the halter on the horse's head and tied the lead rope to the hay rack over the feed trough. She managed to get the bandages off, despite Sugar's frequent stomping of that hoof. But when she tried to get the mare to pick up her foot so Amber could put it in the bucket of by then, lukewarm water, they had a tugging war, and the horse won. Amber tumbled back into the shavings and landed on something squishy and smelly.

Yuck.

"Sugar, please help me here," she begged, when she stood up. She looked at the apple clock. Good thing she'd gotten an early start, but she needed to get this little job done. *Now I'll have to add a shower to my to-do list*, she thought as she felt her wet jeans stick to her backside. "Why were you so good for Mick but not me?"

She bent over and tried again to get the horse to pick up her foot. After more stubbornness on the mare's part, she did. Amber grabbed the bucket of water and quickly shoved it under Sugar's raised hoof, then pulled it down into the bucket. The water wasn't even warm anymore.

Amber squatted down to hold Sugar's leg in the water then looked up at the clock. If she didn't hurry, she'd be late. She still needed to apply the medicine and rewrap—

Sugar must have sensed Amber's distracted thoughts, for she yanked her leg out of the bucket, which knocked it over spilling water everywhere.

Amber jumped up. "What a mess! Darn horse! Why can't you cooperate!" she yelled at the mare. Sugar threw her head up, strained at the rope and snorted. Her eyes looked wide and wild.

As quickly as Amber's temper flared, it receded and she felt terrible about yelling at the poor horse. It wasn't Sugar's fault Amber was inexperienced. She patted the horse's neck and felt like crying. "I'm so sorry, Sugar. Maybe I should call Mandy and see if she..." What was she thinking? This was her job, not Mandy's. She shouldn't rely on the teenager, she was the one getting paid to take care of these animals. Besides, what could Mandy do on crutches? "We'll just have to skip the hoof soaking for now and go on to the rest," she told the mare. Amber wiped her hands on her pant legs and pulled her phone out of her pocket. She didn't usually take it with her to the barn, but with the move, she figured she should be available for her family if they called. She tapped out her parents' number and waited impatiently for someone to answer.

"Are you on your way?" her mom asked.

"No. That's why I called. I'm running a little late."

"Oh, for Heaven's sakes, Amber. Everyone is ready finally and we were just about to leave for Seattle." Her normally calm mother sounded exasperated. Amber wondered if the houseful of family might be getting to her.

"I'm sorry, Mom. I really appreciate everybody's help."

"When will you be there at your apartment?" her mother asked as though she hadn't heard the apology.

"Um...about an hour and a half?" *If the traffic cooperates*, she thought to herself. She didn't dare say that to her mother.

Silence.

"Mom? Are you still there?"

"All right, Amber, we'll see you then," her mother replied with a sigh.

Oh great, Amber thought as she disconnected. *Now my mom's mad at me.*

To Amber's surprise and delight, the traffic headed south on I-5 seemed light with no major delays, and she got to Seattle in the time she'd promised her mother. The move went well and after she'd picked up her mail—including her final paycheck, finally—and handed in her keys to the manager, the entire family went out to dinner. Her dad must have realized that her mom needed a night off from cooking. Amber felt sure her sister-in-law helped as much as possible, but with two young sons probably not a lot. Amber could see the signs of strain on her mother's face at having so many people clutter up her house. And now she'd added to it. When she saw how much space her boxes and furniture took up in the garage, and that her dad moved his car out to the driveway, Amber vowed to herself to get them out of there as soon as possible.

She'd hoped to talk to Brenda during the move to see if the experienced horsewoman could give her any suggestions about getting Sugar's cooperation, but Brenda worked Sunday and didn't join the rest of the family until dinner at the restaurant. And then of course, she sat next to Blake, but Amber sat clear down on the other side of the table by her nephews, and Max claimed all her attention. She finally nabbed Brenda as her dad paid the bill and the rest of the family waited by the door. Amber told her briefly about the situation.

"Sounds like you're doing a great job to me, Amber," Brenda told her. "I'm really proud of you for all you've done there. You've only been working there for, what, two weeks now?" Amber nodded. "Man, you're a fast-learner."

Amber smiled and felt a warm glow flood through her from the praise. *And to think, I used to dislike Brenda.* But then, she frowned. "Funny you should say that. I've heard that before, but I still have trouble believing it sometimes. I mean, look at this whole thing with Sugar. Mick doesn't have any problem getting her to pick up her foot. Why won't she do it for me?"

"Horses have a good sense for the way people feel. I think she can tell you don't have experience with that kind of thing. Be firm with her."

When she headed back to the mini-farm that night, the traffic was nowhere near as sparse as that morning. "Come on, come on," she said aloud to the cars around her as they slowed to a crawl. "I have to get home." Home? She'd thought it again. Well, why not? She really didn't have any other home now.

Chapter Twelve

Amber rushed through the evening feeding starting with the outdoor animals and then cats and dogs. She felt exhausted from the day of moving, but needed to go back out to the barn and check on Sugar. She'd been too busy when she got back to do anything other than feed.

She felt appalled at what she found. The stall was extremely wet from the morning's tipped over bucket of water, and dirty, and the bandages hung loose around Sugar's hoof.

"Oh no," she said to the horse. "I'm supposed to keep your foot clean." She looked around the barn until she spied the pitchfork and an empty five-gallon bucket. She couldn't possibly manage to get out the wheelbarrow, scoop up all the bedding, wade through the mud in the dark—and possibly get stuck—dump the wheelbarrow contents and go back for a load or two of clean shavings. She'd just have to improvise and get up early the next morning to do it right.

After she'd cleaned the stall as much as possible without the wheelbarrow and hauled several buckets of shavings in, Amber dragged herself back to the house. She felt so tired she could barely move. All her earlier good feelings about her caretaking ability vanished.

When Amber staggered out of bed Sunday morning, she dreaded the thought of what she needed to do. She'd have to clean Sugar's stall, and probably Spice's as well since she still left him in at night to keep Sugar company. She dragged her feet, and found one thing after another to do in the house until she couldn't put it off any longer.

This time, she looked in Sugar's stall first, and wished she hadn't. The bandages were completely off, and Sugar stood on only three legs.

Should she call Mick?

Amber ran back into the house, picked up her cell phone and found Mick's number in the Recent Calls list. She tapped on it and waited while it rang and rang than picked up. "Mick, it's Amber..." she began until she realized the voice on the other end was a recording. Should she leave a message? No.

As she tried to decide what to do, Bruiser barked outside. She looked out the windows and saw a truck on the other side of the front gate. Mick must have got her call after all, even though she hadn't left a message. She put the phone down on the island counter and hurried outside.

"Bruiser! Samantha!" Amber called to the dogs.

"I got your call. What's the matter?" Mick asked when he reached her.

"Sugar is worse, and it's all my fault!" Amber exclaimed and felt the tears well up in her eyes. "Yesterday morning, I couldn't get her to soak her foot in the bucket, and so I just put the medicine on and rewrapped it. I don't think I did a very good job of that either. When I looked at it this morning, the bandages had fallen down and wrapped around her ankle. But worse, she's only standing on three legs." She looked down, not wanting to see Mick's disappointment in her on his face.

"Okay, well let's go take a look," Mick said calmly and putting his hand on her shoulder, headed to the barn. When they reached Sugar's stall, Mick grabbed the rope and halter off the half-door, then opened it and walked in. He spoke to the mare in soothing tones as he put the halter on her head. Then he turned and handed the rope to Amber.

She watched anxiously while he bent over, and then knelt down in the shavings to feel Sugar's leg and hoof with his hands. "How is she? Is it bad? Did I make her worse?" She fired questions at him when he stood up again.

"No, I think she'll be okay. How about I help you soak her hoof this time? That should help. I wouldn't be surprised if she improved immensely after that."

She sighed in relief that she hadn't made things any worse for the poor horse. And she wanted to see Mick, but not under these circumstances. "That would be great," she told him. "If you could just show me again, I'm sure I'll get the hang of it."

"I think so too." His smile reassured her

"I'll go get the warm water," she said. When she got back to the barn, she found Mick with Sugar out of the stall and cross-tied in the aisle. She stood there for a moment, and then spoke. "I suppose she picked up her foot—"

"Hoof."

"—Hoof for you."

"Yeah, but then I've been doing this for a long time." Again, Mick seemed to be trying to reassure her.

"True."

"Have you cleaned out Spice's hooves yet?" Mick asked casually. "Remember, I told you a barefoot horse still needs its hooves cleaned every week?"

Oh no, she'd forgotten. One more thing to make her feel inept in front of him.

He must have seen her downcast eyes. "But that was the day I met you and you've had so much to learn, you probably forgot." He grinned.

Why was he giving her excuses? Before she could say anything, he said in a soft voice, "You really have done a tremendous job here, Amber."

What?

"Are you kidding?" she asked him in disbelief.

"No, seriously. From what I can see, you took on this job without any background or experience in farm life and you've done a great job taking care of these animals."

"But, Sugar—"

"Well, as I see it, that's above and beyond. I'm sure no one expected anything like this to happen. I bet Bob and Nancy are just grateful to find someone to step in so quick after Mandy's accident. They're lucky you agreed to take the job. Don't be so hard on yourself."

Amber couldn't believe what she'd just heard—and especially from an experienced horseperson's lips. The worries that had weighed her down since she'd lost her job at the law firm and then taken on this job, seemed to slowly fade. She stood up a little taller and it felt as though the stress in her shoulders and clenched jaw melted away.

"Will you please show me how you get Sugar to pick up her fo—hoof?" She walked over to where the horse stood and leaned over to get a closer look as Mick ran his hand down the mare's leg to her hoof. Before he could even do anything more, it seemed to Amber, Sugar lifted her hoof.

Mick looked up at her. "Ready?" He remained crouched down, and Amber joined him there. "Give me your hand," he said and held his out to her. She gave him her right hand and let him put her fingers around Sugar's ankle. "Now, give her a little squeeze there around her fetlock. Like this, see?" He put his hand over her fingers and squeezed. Sugar lifted her foot. "Now, you try it," he said.

Amber didn't want to hurt Sugar, so she barely put any pressure on the horse's leg…foot…fetlock.

"Try it again, and squeeze a little harder this time," Mick said in an encouraging tone of voice, so Amber did. Sugar's hoof popped up. "See? You're a pro now." He held out his fist to her and she used her left hand to bump knuckles with him.

Amber knew she must be grinning ear to ear like a fool, but she didn't care. But before her head could swell too much, she glanced over at the bucket. "I suppose you want me to put her foot in it."

Mick grinned. "You seem to be on a roll. Go ahead and give it a try," he told her, gesturing to the bucket and then the horse. He stood at the mare's head and talked to her in a low voice, while Amber crouched down next to her again.

"Come on, Sugar, don't make me look bad," she whispered to the mare. As she reached out to grab her fetlock, Sugar lifted her hoof right up. Amber quickly slid the bucket over with one hand while she held Sugar's leg with the other.

"Now, slowly pull her hoof down," Mick said in a quiet voice, but loud enough that she heard him. "And if she resists just hang on." Amber did as he told her, and watched with glee when the mare allowed her to place her foot in the warm water. "Don't let go," Mick warned her.

Amber didn't even care that she had to crouch there for twenty minutes. She whispered to the horse, "Good girl, Sugar. Good girl."

The time sped by and Amber did the rest of the treatment, applying the medicine and then the bandages. Mick asked to switch places toward the end when Sugar, tired of standing in one spot, got fussy. He showed her how to wrap the bandages tight enough so that they wouldn't fall off, but not too tight to cut off circulation in her leg.

Amber felt pretty beat after Mick put the horse back in her cleaned stall and took off her halter, but she remembered what he'd said earlier. "I need to clean Spice's hooves now." She reached for the can of grain and his halter. "Thanks for all your help, Mick. I really appreciate it. I hope I didn't ruin your plans for the day.

"No, just studying. I needed a break." He smiled. "If you want, I'll catch Spice for you." He held out his hand for the halter and attached lead rope.

"Okay, thanks. But I'll clean his hooves. As you said, I'm on a roll." She grinned. "Need the grain?"

"Nah, he knows I carry horse treats in my pocket." He pulled one out and offered it to Sugar, who took it greedily and gobbled it down, then reached out her long head for another. "Berry flavor." He gave her the rest in his hand.

Amber prepared herself for a struggle with Spice, but he surprised her. He lifted his hoof as soon as she touched it. Mick showed her how to use the hoof pick and when she finished that one, she put his hoof back down and headed to his back one. Even before she got there, he lifted it. Amber laughed in delight.

"Look at that. You've got him trained." Mick laughed too.

Amber looked up at him. "I don't think so."

"Yeah, you're right. He does it for me too. But you didn't know that and you have him convinced you know what you're doing. Horses aren't stupid. They know if you don't know what you're doing or are afraid of them."

"Well, that's only because you showed me

what to do. You're a good teacher."

"Then as your teacher, I give you an A plus."

When Amber finished, Mick let Spice back into the pasture, and she got out the pitchfork and wheelbarrow to clean his stall. Mick stayed and chatted with her while she worked, and then helped bring some fresh shavings in for the stalls. Then he looked at his watch and said, "I'd better get back and hit the books, but I can come back in the morning."

"Oh you don't have to do that, Mick. I can handle it now." She could have kicked herself after she said it; he wouldn't have a reason to come by.

"Yeah, I'm sure you can, but maybe I want to. Anyway, I told you I have to check on 'my horses' once in awhile." He grinned mischievously.

"Oh you—" She reached out to him and he must have thought she'd hit him, as he grabbed her hand. But instead of holding her away, he gently pulled her to him. His gaze locked on hers. Then his arms went around her.

Amber felt as though she was held against a wall of muscle. He felt warm and...good, and she knew her heart must be racing as he lowered his head. Then she felt the gentle pressure of his mouth on hers and knew that if he hadn't been holding her so close, her knees might have given way. She knew that she shouldn't, but she wanted the kiss to go on and on. It just felt...right. But she felt his lips leave hers and she wanted to protest.

He traced her jawline with one finger and then, taking her face in both hands, pressed a slow, soft kiss against her lips again. This time, when he pulled back, he smiled and just held her for a few minutes his head resting on hers, before he finally released her altogether. "I'm sorry. I have to go," he said with a look of regret on his face. "See you tomorrow morning?" he asked as he stepped away.

"Yes, I'd like that." She watched him walk to the gate, open it and then climb into his truck. As he drove away, he lifted his hand in a wave.

She smiled.

Chapter Thirteen

Amber felt so psyched about her success with the horses, and the way her relationship with Mick seemed to be headed, she needed to tell somebody. She still hadn't heard from any of her friends since she moved north. Out of sight, out of mind? She wanted to talk to someone who could appreciate how big a deal it was.

She could tell Mandy, but she didn't want to talk to the teenager. She'd probably tell everyone she knew in the area's horse community. Besides, they weren't exactly friends. So once again, she turned to Brenda.

She decided to text in case Brenda might be busy at work: *Call me. Not an emergency.* While she waited for a reply, she made up a list of things she needed from the store. A few minutes later, her cell phone let her know someone was calling. She looked at the screen.

"Hi Brenda. Thanks for calling back. Can you talk for awhile?" she asked.

"Yeah, I'm on a break. What's up?"

Amber gave her the update on Sugar.

"I've been wondering how that worked out, but I didn't get a chance to call you. That's great, Amber. I'm proud of you." Before Amber could talk about her news, Brenda continued on, "I'm glad you called. I've been wanting to ask you something."

Amber wanted to talk about Mick, but she curbed her impatience. "Sure."

"I wondered if you'd like to be in a wedding in June?"

What? All she could think about right now was Mick.

"Your brother and I hope that you'll be a bridesmaid in our wedding," Brenda continued.

"Of course. I'd be happy to."

"Great. Well now that's settled, maybe we can get together soon. My friend Deeann is my maid of honor. I'd like to get your dresses picked out." They chatted a little more about when they could get together and where, and then Brenda said," Oh gee, where did the time go? I have to get back and give Deeann her break. We'll talk again soon, okay?"

"Uh, sure. Bye," Amber said into the phone as Brenda ended the call. Disappointed they hadn't talked about Mick, she sighed, finished her list, grabbed her purse and headed out the door.

Before she went to the grocery store, Amber stopped at the feed store. Mick said she could get the horse treats there, so she hoped they were open on Sunday. When she pulled into the parking lot, she felt relieved to see someone walk out the store's door. She hoped the treats might give Spice and Sugar continued incentive to cooperate with her.

She wandered around the store and looked at the western clothes. There were the gorgeous cowboy boots she'd admired. Just for the heck of it, she decided to try them on. This time she found a place to sit. The boots were a perfect fit. She stood up and walked around a bit. They felt so comfortable too. With regret, she pulled them off, put them back on the shelf and headed to the section for dogs and cats. She'd decided to pick up something for Bruiser and Samantha and the cats too. She didn't know what kind of treats to get the other animals and she needed to make sure she'd have enough money for her groceries, so she stopped browsing, picked up the treats and walked toward the checkout counter.

As she approached, she heard familiar voices. She stopped and looked across the counter to the other side. It was Mardie and Diane, Mick's customers she'd met at Johnny's. She waited for them to look up and say hello, but when she heard Mardie's words, she walked over to a display rack and pretended to be browsing as she shamelessly listened to their discussion.

"I heard Mick plans to take Buck to the Trail Course Event at the Saddle Club this weekend. That should be something to see," Mardie said. "Are you going?"

"I wasn't planning to, but you know, I think that's a good idea. Simba could use some work before we go to the next show. How about you?" Diane answered.

"Are you kidding? Of course. I wouldn't miss a chance to see Mick do his magic with that mustang."

"Are you sure it's the horse you plan to keep an eye on, or the man?" Diane asked and laughed.

"What do you think?" Mardie replied with a

question. "That guy's hot and I'm sure he'll realize what a babe I am sooner or later. I have plans for that man." Amber wouldn't be surprised if the woman leered too.

"What about that Amber he was with at Johnny's? I haven't seen him with anyone in awhile."

"That city gal?" she scoffed. "She's just a new toy for him. He'll get tired of her quick. And guess who will be there waiting for him? I tell you, Diane…"

Amber strained to hear, but the two women's voices faded and she figured they must have paid for their purchases and left. She peeked around the display and saw them walk out the door. As she walked up to the counter, she felt limp like a deflated balloon. She quietly paid for the treats, barely responding to the cheerful saleswoman, and then walked out the door to the parking lot. She didn't think she even had the energy to shop for groceries. She'd just go back to town tomorrow.

As she drove back to the farm, all Amber could think about was how wrong she'd been to make anything out of his kisses. What made her think Mick could be interested in her? She didn't ride horses and show them or participate in any horse events. Why would he want her when horsewomen like Mardie and Diane were after him?

Was she just a new toy to him?

She was glad she hadn't talked about Mick to Brenda after all. His kisses meant nothing.

Amber moped around for awhile when she

got back to the house, but watching Samantha and Bruiser play tag brought her out of it, and she decided to cook a good dinner for herself for a change.

Amber didn't wait for Mick to get there the next morning. She rose earlier than usual and headed out to the barn to feed first thing, and then went back inside the house to feed the dogs, cats and herself. When she figured Sugar must be at least half way through breakfast, Amber went back out to the barn with the bucket of hot water. She knew it would cool down to warm by the time she needed it.

Amber greeted the horse, and then slipped the halter over her head. Sugar protested a bit at being taken away from her food, but Amber pulled a berry-flavored treat out of her pocket and offered it to the mare. That caught Sugar's attention and she agreed to leave the stall as Amber fed her more.

Once she had Sugar cross-tied in the aisle, Amber crouched down and began the process of unwrapping the bandages. She was so intent on it that she didn't realize Mick arrived, until Sugar whickered at his approach.

"How's it going?" Mick asked when he reached them.

Amber wanted to ignore him, but knew she should say something. However, she didn't look up when she spoke. "I don't know yet. I just got started. But at least she was standing on all fours when I got out here."

"Have you had any problems with her?"

"No, I bought some treats at the feed store."

"Ah."

Neither of them said anything else for awhile as Amber finished unwinding the bandages and then asked Sugar to pick up her hoof. Maybe the horse sensed Amber's nervousness, as she refused to lift it at first. Amber continued to apply pressure and Sugar finally gave in. "Good girl," Amber praised her as she shoved the bucket under and then lowered the mare's hoof into the warm water. Amber didn't *want* to look up at Mick then, but she wanted to share her success, and he was the only one who knew how much it meant to her. She grinned at him and he gave her a thumbs-up.

"Good job." He smiled back at her.

Then Amber remembered that she shouldn't care what he thought. Her smile faded and she looked down again. She worked in silence, talking only to the mare, which might have made her feel uncomfortable if she hadn't been busy.

"Need any help?" Mick broke the silence.

"No, I've got it, thanks." Maybe he would take the hint and leave.

"Yes, I can see that. Well, I guess I'll just go to my first appointment then. They'll be shocked to see me on time for once." He laughed, but it sounded forced to her ears

"Okay. See ya."

"Yeah, see ya." Amber heard his steel-toed boots as he walked across the concrete floor. She looked up.

"Mick?"

He stopped at the doorway. "Yeah?"

"Thanks for coming by to help."

He nodded and walked out the door.

Amber sighed. Well that was that. She felt sure he wouldn't come by again. She should feel good about that. She wasn't anyone's toy. She didn't need him. She didn't need any man. If she could handle this job, she could handle anything.

So why did a single tear trickle down her cheek?

****

Mick drove away with a feeling of confusion. What just happened? It seemed as though Amber was mad at him. He couldn't recall that he'd said or done anything to annoy her. He'd even encouraged her. He'd thought about asking her why, but held back. Women. Normally, he wouldn't let something like this bother him…but this time it did.

****

After Mick left, Amber felt determined to forget about her disappointment over him and concentrate on her job search. She opened her laptop up on the island counter in the kitchen. She still hadn't received any calls back for interviews, so she decided to broaden her search somewhat. She'd picked up the local weekly paper in town the day before, and just for fun, she looked at the classified section under Jobs.

There wasn't much to look at. She read help wanted ads for Caretaker, Convenience Store Clerk, Dump Truck Driver, Farmhand, Office Manager/Paralegal for Small Law Firm…Wait. It was the same ad she'd seen before and dismissed. Maybe she should reply. It might be good practice for a job she really wanted. Couldn't hurt. Hmm. No email to reply to, just phone and fax numbers. She grabbed her cell phone and punched in the phone number. It rang several times before someone finally picked up on the other end.

"Hello? Uh, Forbes and Foster," an older man's voice said.

"Hi. I'm calling about the ad for an office manager/paralegal," Amber said. The man didn't reply and she heard a loud bang, then nothing else. She wondered if he'd slammed the phone down. Then she heard a voice again.

"Doggone it. I hate these things…Oh, sorry. Yes. This is Mr. Forbes. I'm one of the partners here. When can you come in and talk to me?"

"Oh. Uh, will tomorrow work for you?" she asked him, momentarily floored that someone wanted to interview her finally. "Afternoon would be better."

"Yes. Two o'clock?" he asked.

"I'll be there. Oh," she said again. "My name is Amber Preston." He gave her directions which she scribbled on the newspaper, but figured she'd use her GPS anyway, since she didn't know the street names.

When the call ended, Amber couldn't hold back a smile of victory. Of course she wouldn't take the job if offered, but at least she'd get some good interviewing experience.

Chapter Fourteen

Amber, dressed in her power interview suit, parked her car at the curb in front of the law offices of Forbes and Foster. She flipped down the sun visor and looked in the mirror as she applied some lipstick, then wiped the excess from her lips with a tissue. She couldn't believe how nervous she felt about an interview she didn't really care about. She told herself again that it was merely a dress rehearsal for the real thing, and she needed to relax. She did a couple shoulder shrugs to loosen up her tense neck muscles, and then got out of the car, automatically hit the remote for the alarm—though it probably wasn't necessary in the small town—and headed for the office.

When she opened the door, no one greeted her. She walked up to the reception counter.

"Hello?" No answer. She peered around the counter and saw a room with a desk, but no one there. She took a few steps forward and saw a hallway to the right that lead to a couple offices and restrooms. "Hello?"

Suddenly, a door she hadn't noticed slammed open and an older man with an armload of manila files walked through. "Oh." He seemed startled when he looked up and saw her there.

"Mr. Forbes?"

"Yes. How can I help you?"

"I'm Amber Preston. I'm here for the interview."

"Oh yes. Follow me, please." He led the way to one of the offices down the short hallway, and when they entered, he gestured to a chair. "Please sit down. Do you have your resume?" he asked as he sat down in a chair on the other side of the desk.

Much later, Amber felt surprised when she looked down at her lap and glanced at her watch. She and the attorney talked for forty-five minutes, and it seemed like no time at all. She heard the front door open and footsteps come at a brisk pace down the hall.

"Greg? Is that you?" Mr. Forbes called.

"Yup, it's me, Dave," a deep voice answered. A tall, dark-haired man, much younger than Mr. Forbes, paused in the doorway of the office. He smiled at Amber. "Hello. Are you here for the interview?"

"Yes. I'm Amber Preston." She held out her hand and the man took it.

"Good to meet you. I'm Greg Foster, the other partner." He took her resume that Mr. Forbes handed to him across the desk, and briefly scanned it, then looked up again. "Do you have any questions about the job?"

Amber tried to recall the questions she'd prepared, but none of them seemed appropriate. She knew it was too soon to ask about salary, so she asked about the previous office manager/paralegal and why that person left the job.

"Yes, well..." he looked at Mr. Forbes. When the older man nodded, he turned back to Amber and continued. "We've had some recent changes in staffing. A former partner left to open his own firm and she went with him." He looked around. "I suppose Dave told you we have a part-time receptionist who is here in the mornings. So with you—or the person we hire for the job—there are just the four of us. I see you came from a large firm in Seattle. Would a small office be a problem for you?" Greg asked her.

"No," she blurted out without thinking. She didn't know why, but she felt comfortable there. And the job, no matter what it paid, would be a step up in experience for her, and look good on her resume.

Greg—Mr. Foster—looked at Mr. Forbes again and then back at her. Then Mr. Forbes cleared his throat. "Well, if you don't have any more questions, Greg, I think we'd better let this young lady go. I have a trial to prepare for." He stood up and Amber did the same. "Let me show you around the office on your way out," he said. Amber took that as a good sign.

After the short tour, she and Mr. Forbes shook hands and she walked out the door to her car. She had a good feeling about the interview as she drove back to the farm. Of course it was just for practice, but she found herself wishing she could take the job. If only it was in Seattle.

Chapter Fifteen

The next day, Amber got online again and searched her regular jobsites. Then she remembered that she'd not heard back from Sally Goodwin at Templeton and Howe. Maybe if she showed she was really interested in the job, it would make up for missing the phone interview. She found the number on her phone and pressed it. As the phone rang, she rehearsed what to say. This time she wouldn't just leave a message on the woman's voicemail.

"Good morning, Templeton and Howe. How may I direct your call?" a pleasant voice answered the phone on the other end of the line.

"Sally Goodwin, please," Amber said back. But when the receptionist connected her to Sally's line, all she got was the voicemail again. She hung up and called the number again. This time when the receptionist answered, Amber said, "Can you tell me if the paralegal position has been filled?"

"Um…yes, I believe so. Please hold while I check." Amber heard some muffled voices and then the receptionist spoke into the phone. "Yes, it's been filled. Can I help you with anything else?"

"No. That's it. Thanks." Amber ended the call. Well, what had she expected? Small town Forbes and Foster looked more and more appealing all the time.

Half an hour later, Amber's phone rang. She looked at the area code and saw it was a Seattle number. "Hello?"

"Hello Amber, this is Sally Goodwin returning your call."

That was a surprise, and especially since the job had been filled. "Oh, hi. I called to see if you'd filled the paralegal position, but I understand you did."

There was a bit of a hesitation on the other end of the line, but then the women spoke again. "Yes, that's correct. However, it didn't work out and I am setting up interviews. Are you interested?"

Was the woman kidding? No, she didn't sound like the type. "Yes, I am," Amber answered in a calm, professional voice, though inside she wanted to shout, 'Of course!'

"Can you come in tomorrow, say…two o'clock?"

What was it with these law firms and two o'clock? It would put her right into rush hour coming back. But beggars couldn't be choosers, her dad always said. "Yes, I can," she replied.

"Great. We'll see you then." The woman gave her the address and told her where to park, and hung up.

"I have an interview in Seattle at last!" Amber told the cats with a whoop. They ignored her and continued their naps. "It's a good thing I did that interview with Forbes and Foster. Good practice. This will be a breeze," she enthused to the cats anyway. "Oh." Her smile faded. She'd liked that place, the friendly attorneys, the slower pace of the small town law firm…What was she thinking? As Mardie said, she was a city girl. She belonged in a downtown Seattle law firm…didn't she?

When Amber came back from Seattle the next evening, she wasn't so sure. The hour she spent at the law firm brought back memories of her previous job. Everyone was in a hurry. No one smiled. She could feel the tension in the place. The paralegals looked stressed and tired and when she asked about overtime, the paralegal she spoke to, frowned at her before she answered. "Well of course we all work Saturdays and often after hours during the week. But you'll be compensated of course." As though money was all that mattered. In other words, the job would take over her life again. Could she see herself doing that for the rest of her working days until she retired—or died of a heart attack?

When the phone rang, she thought it might be Sally Goodwin. So what if it was seven o'clock at night? The woman probably worked as long as everyone else in the place.

She picked up the phone and answered, dispiritedly, "Hello?"

"Hi Amber, it's Mick."

Mick?

"So." He seemed hesitant, not at all the Mick she knew. "How are you doing? Has Sugar been behaving for you?"

Amber laughed nervously. "She was a little stubborn, but I think we have an understanding now. I bribe her and she lets me do what I want."

"Well good. That's great. I'm glad you two are getting along so well."

"Yeah. So, how are you?" she asked politely. "Are you getting to your appointments on time?"

Mick laughed. "Nah, I'm back to my usual. But my clients are used to it. If I get there on time, they aren't ready." He paused again. How's your job search going? Did you ever give any thought to looking locally?"

"Funny you should ask. I did. In fact, I had an interview at Forbes and Foster in town."

"That's fantastic, Amber," he told her. "Way to go. Do you think they'll offer you the job?"

"I don't know. But it was good practice." She hesitated this time, unsure what to say next. "I, uh, also had an interview with a law firm in Seattle today."

"Oh." His voice sounded flat, as though he might be disappointed. Could it be that maybe she wasn't just a new toy to him? That he had some kind of feelings for her too?

"But I haven't heard back. In fact, I thought when you called just now that it might be their human resources person."

He paused again. "Say, I know you aren't especially interested in riding—"

"I never said that. In fact, I'd thought about asking you for a lesson, but then this whole thing with Sugar came up and I've been busy…"

"Yes, you have. You'd like a lesson, huh?" He sounded surprised.

"Well, yeah, I've been thinking about it," she replied. "Spending all this time around Sugar, I feel a lot less nervous around horses. I think it might be fun to learn to ride."

"I'd be happy to teach you." He sounded pleased and more like the Mick she knew. "I don't want to push you or anything, but do you want to come over this weekend?" He paused again. "Oh yeah, it'll have to be Sunday. Buck and I are going to a trail course event this Saturday. It's a fundraiser for the local equestrian trails."

She didn't plan to tell him she'd already heard he was going to the event. Then she'd have to tell him *why* she knew. "What do you do there? I heard some people talking about it at the feed store."

"Take my horse over and through obstacles that we might find on the trail when we're out riding or in trail classes at horse shows. You know, things like opening gates, riding over a bridge, or through water. Or other things that are scary to horses, like tarps, putting on a raincoat, and flags flapping in the breeze. In a trail class, the horse and rider are timed at how quickly they go through the course," he explained.

"That sounds interesting. I've never been to anything like that," she said wistfully.

"Would you like to?" She'd caught him by surprise again.

"Yeah. I think it would be fun. Maybe I'll go to one sometime."

"How about this Saturday? Buck and I can pick you up, or you can meet us at my place."

"You want me to come with you?" she asked.

"Would I ask you if I didn't?" This time he sounded baffled, as though he couldn't believe she would doubt his sincerity. "Of course I do. Besides, you'd be doing me a favor. Maybe when she sees you there, that Mardie will quit bugging me." He sighed. "I'm sure she'll be there—and the rest of her bunch."

Now it was her turn to be surprised. "Are you sure you don't want to hang out with her?"

"If I did, I would have asked her to come with me. I asked you."

"I don't know much about horses, you know." She just had to say it.

"You know enough," he replied.

After they'd determined she'd meet him at his place, he'd given her his address, and the call ended, Amber just sat there. How had she gotten such a wrong idea about Mick? She'd assumed he'd rather be around horsewomen.

Amber came back from her day with Mick and Buck thoroughly exhausted—and happy. She thought she'd feel awkward and out of place around all the horses and their riders, but she didn't. She felt…accepted. Mick introduced her to everyone, and explained where she worked and why, so whether because she was with him or because of Bob and Nancy—who everyone she talked to seemed to know and like—she didn't know. But it didn't matter. She'd even been asked to help out with some of the trail obstacles, setting them up when a horse knocked them down, and exchanging good-natured banter with the other course helpers.

Mick asked if she wanted to ride Buck around a bit, but she told him she'd wait until her lesson the next day. With so many other horses and people milling around, she thought the horse might get too excited and buck her off or something. She preferred her first real horse ride take place in a quieter setting and without an audience. But she did lead him around and took him to graze once Mick removed his saddle at the end of the day. He was a beautiful horse and very gentle.

Amber ran her hand down his long face, from the white star on his forehead to his soft nose. "You're very handsome, you know. I'm sure all the mares think you're a hottie." The horse jerked his head up.

"Are you two talking about me?" Mick's voice came from behind her.

"Such an ego. No, actually I told him how good he looked out there on the course." She turned and smirked at him.

"What about me?" He gave her a mock hurt look.

"You were okay, I guess..." she teased.

"Oh, I get it. You're buttering him up so he'll let you ride him tomorrow," Mick said in a stage whisper as though he didn't want Buck to hear.

"Oh you." She went to smack him again, but

he grabbed her hand, and pulled her to him.

"Ah-ah, there will be none of that. What will Buck think?"

She opened her mouth to reply, but Mick pulled her firmly to his chest and kissed her full on the lips. The kiss deepened…until she felt a shove from behind. "Buck."

"I think he's jealous." Mick laughed.

"Maybe he's hungry and wants to go home." Amber laughed too.

"You're probably right. Guess we'd better pack up and go," Mick replied, but he sounded regretful, Amber thought. *She* was.

Her riding lesson the next day was a blast. Buck was a perfect gentleman, Mick told her, because the horse liked her.

The feeling was mutual. And of course, there was the added bonus of her riding instructor, who encouraged her as she rode around the circular outdoor arena. She felt glad to see the sandy footing. Maybe it wouldn't hurt so much when she fell, as she felt sure she would.

Mick showed her how to squeeze her legs around the horse and make a clucking noise with her tongue to get Buck started forward. As he walked around the arena, she felt more and more comfortable. Whenever Mick stopped her, he'd place his hand on her knee or thigh as he explained something. The first touch felt electric, and she nearly jumped out of the saddle, but after that, it comforted her as she supposed he meant it to.

And after the lesson, when Mick told her to

kick her feet free of the stirrups and slide down out of the saddle, he was there to catch her…of course it was a long way down to the ground from such a tall horse. Well and that led to a hug and another long kiss.

She could hardly wait for the next lesson.

The next day, Amber felt so stiff, she could barely move. She felt sure she'd used muscles she'd never used before. She dressed slowly and almost tiptoed out the door. Any kind of movement felt like agony. So, this was horseback riding, huh? Why would anyone torture themselves like this time after time? Maybe she'd go back to feeding and petting them. She just wanted to go back to bed, but maybe a good soak in the tub would help. She looked longingly at the hot tub on the back deck. No, too cold for that.

When she got back in the house after she'd fed, anxious to run a bath, she heard her cell phone ringing on the island counter. She rushed over from the entranceway and nearly tripped over Zee to get there. Of course, the cat wanted some love *now*. She gave her a quick pet with one hand, groaned and reached for the phone with the other.

"Hello?" she answered, short of breath.

"Amber?" She didn't recognize the voice.

"Yes."

"Hi, this is Greg Foster from Forbes and Foster."

"Oh, yes. How are you?"

"Well I'm fine, but I'll be even better if you take the officer manager/paralegal job that Dave and I want to offer you." He laughed.

Oh no. She really hadn't expected this. "I, uh…"she hesitated at a loss for an answer.

"I'm not sure if Dave told you what the pay is, but—"

"No, we didn't get around to that," she told him.

"Oh. Well, we're prepared to pay you a little more than we put in the ad…"

She didn't remember seeing any amount in the newspaper ad and looked around for her purse. She must have been so intent on her search, she didn't hear his next words as he named a figure.

"Excuse me, can you say that again? I must have another call coming in. It bleeped out your voice there for a sec." It was just a little white lie. She didn't want him to know she wasn't paying attention.

But when he said the figure again, she was left speechless for a moment.

"Oh, um, that's very generous." How could she turn it down? She *had* to turn him down. "Mr. Foster, I don't mean to appear ungrateful, but I need to think about it."

"Of course. I'm sure you have other offers to consider. How much time do you need?" he asked in a pleasant tone.

Coward. Why didn't she just tell him 'no' now? "Can I have the rest of the week to think about it?"

"Sure. In fact, we'll be out of town on a case on Friday, so how about we talk next Tuesday?"

Amber agreed with relief.

Mick called later that day. "How are you? Any aches and pains?"

Amber groaned.

"That bad, huh? Don't worry, they'll work out. You just need to go riding again," he told her.

"I don't think I ever want to ride again."

"Sure you do. It's fun. Tell you what. When you get done with whatever you're doing, come over here and we'll go on a short trail ride together."

"Hmmm. That does sound tempting. Are you sure it will make me feel better?"

"Oh yeah." She could hear the leer in his voice.

"Well, if you promise…"

"Scout's honor. And you'd be doing me a favor. I need to exercise the mare."

They talked a little more and then Mick asked her what she'd been doing when he called and she told him about the call from Greg Foster.

"When do you have to give them your answer?" Mick asked

"I have to let them know next Tuesday. But Mick, when my job here ends I'll have nowhere to live and I'll have to go back to Seattle."

"Why? I thought you moved out of your apartment there."

"I did."

"There are places to live in Stanwood too, you know. Or Camano or north or south."

"But I'm a city girl," she replied, though even as she said it to him, she heard her voice waver.

"Are you sure?"

"Well...No," she admitted.

Mick proved to be right. After she'd ridden awhile, she loosened up and the heat of the horse's body combined to make her stiffness go away. And of course, there was that pleasant view of that hunk of man riding tall in the saddle leading the way down the trail. And more kisses and hugs after the ride.

By Monday of the next week, they'd managed to get several more rides in—with stops for kisses—before dark fell each night, and she felt perfectly comfortable and capable in the saddle...and with Mick.

Tomorrow, she'd have to give Greg Foster an answer. Amber thought about what Mick said to her. There was nothing keeping her in Seattle and nothing to return to—no apartment and apparently, no friends and maybe not even a job that she wanted. She could visit her family on weekends, her parents in Bellevue and her brothers wherever they lived. But here, she had an actual job offer and a man she'd grown close to and a relationship that promised more. She knew if she went back to working in a Seattle law firm, she'd get all caught up in that lifestyle again, back to being a workaholic with no life and she and Mick would probably drift apart.

Amber's phone rang, startling her out of her

thoughts. "Hello?"

"Amber Preston?"

"Yes."

This is Tami Bradley, Sally Goodwin's assistant at Templeton and Howe."

"Yes, I remember you."

"Ms. Goodwin wants to know if you can come in for an interview tomorrow."

Before she could answer, Amber heard a beep on the line. "Can I put you on hold for a second, Tami? I have to take this other call." She supposed she could have ignored it. She didn't see the caller's number on the screen, but it gave her a moment to think anyway.

"Oh sure, no worries." The young woman sounded bored.

Amber switched to the other call.

"Hi. It's Brenda. Hey, I need to ask you something."

"Okay." Amber supposed Brenda wanted to discuss the wedding and she half-listened, still thinking about the other call waiting."What? Sorry Brenda, I didn't hear you."

"Well, what do you want me to tell them?"

Oh boy. She needed to quit letting her mind drift off when people talked to her. "I'm sorry, Brenda. What was the question again? Tell them what?"

"Didn't you hear anything I said?" Brenda sounded disgruntled and Amber didn't blame her. "I said, Bob called me and asked how you were doing and when I told him about Sugar, Nancy got on the line and asked me about a million questions I couldn't answer, so she's going to call you. By the way, be sure to answer their phone if it rings 'cause it will be her. However, I told them you were handling it, and Bob got back on the phone. They want to extend their vacation a couple weeks or so and want to know if you can stay on awhile longer. So, can you?"

Amber didn't have to think about it. Sometimes you had to take risks in life. "Tell them yes. I'll do it."

"There's more." Brenda sounded hesitant this time.

"What?"

"Well, they might want you to stay a little longer…"

"Brenda, its sounds like you're holding something back. Just say it," Amber told her impatiently

"They might want you to stay even longer…"

"Brenda."

"Okay, they're looking at getting a second home in Arizona and wonder if you'll be available to maybe live there in the RV or something year-'round," she said in a rush as though afraid to ask. "At least for awhile."

"That would be great. I love it here," Amber said and laughed into the phone.

The next afternoon, Amber made a phone call. It rang and rang, and when someone finally picked up, she heard a sound as though the phone dropped on the other end and then, "Doggone it, I hate these things…uh, Forbes and Foster."

After Amber fed the animals that night, she picked up her cell phone and punched in a number. It rang and rang. She thought it might go to voicemail, but then a voice said, "Hello. Amber?"

"I took the job. Wanna go out to dinner and celebrate? I'm buying."

"Give me fifteen minutes and I'll be there to pick you up."

As he disconnected the call, she heard a loud *Whoopée!* and then silence. Mick was on his way.

Chapter Sixteen

When Mick got out of the truck at the restaurant, Amber saw him reach back and pull a box off the back seat before he walked around and opened her door. She no longer needed help getting in or out, but Mick insisted he'd never hear the end of it if his mama caught him making a lady climb out of his pickup. She didn't mind his old-fashioned manners, and she thought maybe she even liked them. For sure, she'd like to meet the woman who taught them to him. And the way Mick hinted, she thought that might be soon.

"What's in that box you've got there, Mick?" she asked him coyly.

"Never you mind. You'll find out soon enough," he answered with a gleam in his eye. He shut the truck door and offered her his hand.

They'd decided on Johnny's for dinner again. Since it was a weeknight, it wasn't quite as crowded this time and they walked right to a table. Again, other diners said hello to Mick, but this time, she heard "Hi Amber" too as she walked past. She smiled and might have stopped to say hello, but Mick seemed to be on a mission. He kept a tight grip on her hand and merely nodded at the greetings.

Mick suggested a spaghetti dinner meal for two this time, and when Amber agreed, the waitress set down their glasses of water and left. Mick held up his glass and touched it to hers in a toast.

"Here's to your new job. Maybe later we can go somewhere for a real toast, but for now, is water okay?"

Amber smiled and nodded. She didn't think she'd stopped smiling since she'd made her decision. She picked up the glass and took a huge, unladylike gulp. When Mick held the box out to her, she didn't think the day could get any better.

"What's this for?" she asked him

"Something I've been wanting to give you and today just seemed...well, go ahead and open it," he urged, sitting back in the chair.

When Amber tore off the wrapping, she smelled leather, and when she saw a bucking bronco on the box, she felt sure she knew what was inside. However, appearances could be deceiving—she knew that from her family that delighted in wrapping Christmas gifts in boxes of various shapes and sizes to fool their recipient until the very last second. Not so this time. Still, she gasped as she pulled off the lid.

"Oh Mick, I thought they were gone! When I went back to the feed store to buy them, they were gone...because you bought them." She pulled the beautiful, soft leather cowboy boots—that would go with everything—out of the box, kicked off her shoes and pulled them on. "How did you know I wanted them?" She reached across the table and grasped his hand in hers.

"You needed a good pair of boots."

"Good things always come in pairs," she told him with a smile.

"Like us." He winked, leaned across the table, and tugged her closer. Their lips met in a kiss.

Suddenly, Amber heard a voice next to their table.

"So…you and Mick, huh?" Mandy laughed. "I can't say I'm surprised. I thought you two would make the perfect pair."

ABOUT THE AUTHOR
MARILYN CONNER MILES

Marilyn began writing as soon as she could print. Her first career was in the transportation industry, working for the airlines. Her second career was in advertising, marketing and promotions. Currently a freelance editor, Marilyn lives with her husband and cat in the foothills of the Cascade Mountains in southwest Washington State, where she watches horses, deer and sometimes owls from her home office window.

Made in the USA
Charleston, SC
20 December 2014